MW00436209

TUMBLEWEED CHRISTMAS

NINIE HAMMON

Sterling & Stone

Chapter One

THE BACK of our cattle truck and the high-walled cotton trailer behind it were as empty as the hollow place in my belly that felt so cold and vacant sometimes it took my breath away.

It bounced along on the uneven asphalt of US 84 that cuts in a knife stroke across eastern New Mexico. Daddy had gotten me up before dawn and I'd dressed in the dark. Driving straight through, we'd be home before midnight.

That was how we got here. Here on this road and here at this point in my life where my world had crumbled away —big hunks just *gone*—until there was almost nothing left of it at all.

"You want to stop for a Coke-Cola?" Daddy asked, fighting the steering wheel to keep the empty truck on the bumpy road.

I shook my head.

"Need to pee?"

Again I shook my head, not trusting myself to speak for fear I'd start crying again. I wouldn't do that, wouldn't give him the satisfaction of knowing how heartbroken I'd been when we found out we'd be deadheading it all the way home, nothing to show for the trip but sore backsides.

"The Gulf Station in Fort Sumner is the last place you'll have to go to the bathroom," he said, like it was news to me there was nothing but prairie between Santa Rosa and Clovis, New Mexico.

The silence settled back around us, broken only by the clicks, clacks and clunks of the old cattle truck bumping along.

I'd liked silence once. It had felt warm and deliciously all mine when I'd get home from school and Mama was in the show ring with her horses or off painting somewhere, and Daddy was out with the cattle and I had the big old house all to myself. I'd sit in the window seat in my loft bedroom overlooking a backyard that stretched out for as far as the eye could see in every direction, all the way to the horizon, flat and barren. Well, not totally barren—there were a few trees here and there that somebody'd planted and watered and babied and prayed over—but mostly my view was of what Spencer called "miles and miles of nothing but miles and miles." And I'd pretend the empty prairie was an ocean and I was the captain of a three-masted Spanish galleon sailing on sparkling water that reached out forever to the blue bowl of sky overhead.

"It's nobody's fault, you know," Daddy said.

Yes, it is. It's your fault—everything's your fault, I wanted to say.

Instead, I turned and looked out the window at the tumbleweeds dancing in the wind, colliding with posts and yucca plants, rushing toward a barbed-wire death smashed against the fences.

"How could anybody know there'd be a snowstorm?"

Blizzard, actually. It would one day be called the Great Blizzard of 1953. High in the Sangre De Cristo Mountains, a vicious storm had dumped almost fifteen feet of snow in less than twelve hours. Roads were blocked by drifts twice as tall as a car, bridges were impassable. The whole landscape was buried under a shimmering white blanket—including the load of Christmas trees we'd driven all the way from Granger County, Texas, to collect.

"I'm talking to you, young lady," he finally snapped. "You act like I'm responsible for the blizzard."

No, he wasn't responsible for the blizzard. But he was responsible for life getting so out of control. For chaos where there had been order. For loose ends dangling everywhere, dentist appointments missed, birthdays forgotten and…and…*no milk for breakfast*. I didn't know what backup plan he should have had when the only source of the whole county's Christmas trees was suddenly buried in a snowdrift. But he should have done *something*. He was in charge and *it was his job to keep the wheels on*.

Then it occurred to me with a sudden sense of triumph that Daddy was the man who'd screwed this up. Nobody could argue that. This time I wouldn't be the only person mad at him. Now, maybe the whole county would hate him as much as I did.

When we got to the house, I hopped down out of the cattle truck and raced inside, deposited my coat on the hook by the door, and barreled up the stairs to my room. I didn't slam the door, though I wanted to, just threw myself on my bed and let go, releasing the tears I'd been holding back for hundreds of miles.

No Christmas tree.

On the way home, bouncing along for hours in the cattle truck, all the awful in my life had morphed together into this one thing, and grieving for the loss of a tree was grieving for it all, for all the losses, for all the things that had been warm and comfortable and good that were now gone forever.

Daddy could even ruin Christmas!

My bedroom was always cold in the wintertime, tucked up under the eaves of the house, but I could hear the protesting clanking in the heat registers that meant Daddy'd turned on the furnace. Crying was exhausting and I was already worn out. After a while, I was vaguely aware of Daddy standing in the open doorway, but I was no longer sobbing the great wrenching sobs that made my chest ache. By then, I was just making pitiful little squeaking sounds like a baby jackrabbit run over by a combine. He didn't make me get up, take my shoes off and put on my pajamas, though. He just stepped into the room and pulled the scrap quilt his mother had made over my shoulders and tucked it under my chin. I pretended I didn't notice and kept my eyes squeezed shut as long as I could sense his presence in the room. He stood beside my bed for a long time, not saying anything. Then he either left or I fell asleep, because the next thing I knew it was morning.

Chapter Two

THE MANURE DIDN'T MAKE contact with the ventilation system, as Spencer would have put it, right away. It took a while for news of the no-trees calamity to filter out to the outlying farms and ranches and for the enormity of the loss to sink in. Everyone floated blissfully down Denial River for a time, assuming *somebody* would do something, find some trees somewhere else or…well, *something.* When I heard kids on the school bus talking about it right before Christmas break, I knew the pot was about to boil over.

"Mama says we're not gonna have a Christmas tree this year." That was Gretchen Oliver. Her mother was known as the Harbinger of Doom, so Gretchen had come by her Chicken Little disposition honestly.

"That's stupid. We always have a tree." Roger Halburton would have argued the point either way. If Gretchen'd said there would be trees, he'd have said there wouldn't.

"Mama says *nobody's* gonna have a tree." Gretchen was not to be denied her hour in the gloom. "She said there was a blizzard, and when they went to get the trees, the man told them they were all covered up with snow."

What the man had said, specifically, was, "Look, pal, you think you can dig 'em out, here's a shovel. Be my guest."

"Ask Bonnie if you don't believe me," Gretchen said, turning to me. "Her daddy's the president of the association." The Granger County Cattlemen's Association—a group of ranchers, farmers and local businessmen—sold Christmas trees every year on the vacant lot next to the Baptist Church, and used the proceeds—if they made a profit and usually they didn't—to buy holiday decorations for the courthouse and downtown buildings.

"We went all the way past Taos and back," I said. "Took us all day. No trees."

"See!" Gretchen said. "Told ya."

"Daddy hasn't tried to get any trees anywhere else, far as I know," I said casually, hoping they'd carry that little morsel home and share it with their parents. In truth, my father had done little else in the days since our fruitless trip to New Mexico. I momentarily considered telling them that he'd said everybody should go out, find themselves a tree and chop it down, but that was going too far. Any idiot knew that cutting down a tree in west Texas, for Christmas or for any other reason, could get you shot.

So I fired out a safer line. "Daddy doesn't care that there aren't any trees. He said it saved him the trouble of trying to untangle the Christmas lights."

Apparently, that tasty tidbit did make it home to be discussed around the dinner table that night because three days later there was an emergency meeting at our house of the board of directors of the Cattlemen's Association.

Chapter Three

DADDY WAS ALWAYS at the house when I got off the bus from school—every day—almost like he was waiting for me, though he never said a word to me and acted like I wasn't even there. Just one more straw to pile on the back of my discontent. One of thousands of reasons I longed for *Before*—that magical, mythical time when the sun shone every day and everybody smiled and the only time I cried was when I skinned my knee. In *Before* I came home to an empty house. It wasn't like I was alone, of course. There were always ranch hands around, and Daddy and Mama were nearby if I needed them. And it wouldn't be long before one or the other of them showed up—usually Mama, carrying in her gigantic art folder what she'd created sitting on some isolated patch of prairie. The lonely tranquility of a windmill. Cattle drinking at a trough. A platoon of fence posts marching away single file into the distance.

Mama usually didn't make it home until late on Wednesdays, though. That was chili day and Mama loved chili, so she'd set up her easel and paint all afternoon in the

Fellowship Hall of the Methodist Church in town, where the women in the Granger County Homemakers' Circle served potluck lunches three times a week. She was a celebrity of sorts there and the few times I went with her, it was like she was holding court with the other women, painting as she talked, rather than having simple conversations. Among them but not one of them, no more suited to the blowing dirt of west Texas than my father had been to the rolling green meadows of Tennessee.

Mama cultivated her differences and I was proud of her for that. She never tried to be like the ladies who'd come there to gossip, talk about embroidery, somebody's new baby, recipes—but mostly to gossip. And to their credit, they didn't appear to expect or even want her to be like them. She was *interesting.* They enjoyed her flamboyance—dressed in flowing Spanish skirts, dangling earrings, turquoise bracelets, lacy shawls and always, always, always wearing tiny splatters of paint like she'd been dusted with colored baby powder.

Though I'd have argued different at the time, in truth my mother wasn't beautiful in any traditional sense. But her features were striking—*she* was striking—with wide hazel eyes, the kind of pouty lips men went all stupid over, an hourglass figure and hair the color of a chestnut foal. It fell all the way to her waist when she took out the pins that kept it piled on top of her head. Though she never wore makeup, every man turned to look at her when she entered a room, and their wives would surely have hated her for that but for two things. One, she wasn't a flirt, oblivious to every other male human being on the planet except my father. And two, hers was a kind and gentle soul. She spoke in a soft voice, listened in rapt attention and looked deeply into the eyes of everyone she met. Not to mention that she probably knew more about horses than anybody for a hundred miles in every direction, which landed her kindred-spirit status with every other Texan.

And then there was the art, of course. She'd been locally famous in Hilton Head, South Carolina, where her parents had a beach house. She'd been conducting an outdoor art show there, in fact, when my father first saw her. He'd joined the Marine Corps three days after Pearl Harbor, was on a ten-day pass after basic training at the Marine base in Parris Island, and spent nine of those days courting my mother. He married Rosemary Elizabeth Cresswell on the tenth, then shipped out for the South Pacific. He didn't see the little girl she named Bonnie Leigh —she had a thing for *Gone With The Wind*—until the war was over.

Mama got her first look at the Texas High Plains then, when he brought us home to the sprawling ranch that had been in his family since his grandfather staked his claim on the homestead in the late 1800s. It wasn't as big as the Four Sixes or the Big K ranches on the other side of Lubbock, of course, but it was by far the biggest ranch in Granger County, so large Daddy could raise cattle on the grasslands and still have plenty of room for several square-mile sections of cotton and grain sorghum.

I once heard Spencer teasing Mama. "Rosie," he'd said —he was the only person who called her that—"the culture shock of you seeing the Big Empty for the first time should have been strong enough to register on the Richter scale."

Oh, she'd gasped at the sight, alright. But not from shock. For Mama and the flat, open prairie, it had been love at first sight.

"Do you have homework to do?" Daddy asked as I let the screen door bang shut behind me because I knew it irritated him. Before I had a chance to answer, he said,

"You can't do it at the kitchen table. We're having company, the association board's meeting here tonight."

With Daddy presiding over the affair, the men wouldn't be treated like company, that was for sure. No little cookies on a crystal platter. No coffee in fancy cups. Mama'd brought her "china" to Texas with her from Tennessee and she never missed an opportunity to use it. Though even I could see the delicate cups looked awkward in the hands of cattlemen like my father, raw boned and hardened by the wind, sun and unrelenting emptiness of High Plains life.

"I'll get my homework done sometime this weekend—Saturday, maybe, or Sunday…sometime," I replied airily, also because I knew it annoyed him.

Jobs were to be done "on time, in order," with the thing you liked to do least first on the list. That was the Corps way. There was no such thing as an *ex*-Marine, and Daddy'd only been home from Korea for ten months. He never talked about it, though. Korea. Never once even said the word. Never talked about his medals, either.

I hadn't even known he had any until I found them, so long ago now, in that period of ancient history I thought of as Back When I Cared.

I can't find the boot polish anywhere! I've turned the whole house upside down. There's nowhere else to look, so if it's not here in Daddy's closet…

*A battered shoebox is tucked back in the far corner of the closet. The lid is taped to the box with Scotch tape, but one piece of the tape has come loose. I move the shoes and boots out of the way and pull the box out into the light, lifting the side of the lid that has come free. At first I don't know what the things inside the box are, pieces of fabric with something attached to the end, something metal—*Medal. *These* are medals, the ones they give to a soldier who's very brave! They're Daddy's medals.

The box is full of them, and I lift each one out carefully and lay it on the hardwood floor beside me. Some look old, like maybe they're from World War II. But most are brand new, medallions hanging from striped or solid-colored ribbons with pins on the other end.

A few of the pieces of metal have words on them.

One at the end of a ribbon that's green, with yellow, blue and white stripes says Korean Defense Service Medal. One just says US Marine Corps, a red ribbon with a blue stripe in the middle and a tiny rifle hanging between the ribbon and the medal. One is a solid purple ribbon with a heart hanging beneath it that has the image of George Washington on it like on a quarter.

All the ribbons are unique. Most are solid colors—green, blue or gold with stripes of different colors and widths on the edges. There are red stripes, thin gold and purple ones and ribbons with a single big stripe in the middle. The medals attached to the ribbons are unique, too—round, square, gold- or bronze-colored with images of guns or eagles or swords.

When I finally dig down to the bottom of the box, there are two new medals lying side by side. I reach out to touch them, but don't for a moment. They give me goose bumps and I don't know why. One is a black ribbon, with thin red, white and blue stripes on the edge. There are no words, but the eagle in the center of the gold medallion hanging below the ribbon is surrounded by what looks like barbed wire. The other has no words on it either. It's just a red, white and blue striped ribbon with a gold star hanging beneath it.

Why did Daddy stuff these in a box in the closet? They ought to be out where you can see them, on the wall maybe—

I freeze. I know what I'll do! I'll frame them and give them to Daddy on Monday for his birthday, instead of the batch of the fudge I was planning to make that would probably taste awful anyway.

Finding a picture frame is simple. Mama had lots of them. Purple velvet is easy to come by, too—my Easter dress from two years *ago that's way too tight now. I get the Elmer's Glue out of the kitchen junk drawer and glue the velvet on one of Mama's blank canvases, put the canvas in a frame and pin the medals to the velvet.*

I can barely sit still through dinner on Monday night. When I give him the gift, wrapped in brown grocery-sack paper, he looks confused, and I realize he doesn't even remember what today is.

"Happy birthday!" I squeal.

He nods then and dutifully rips the paper away to reveal the frame and medals beneath.

There's a breathless pause, like the instant after you scratch a match across that rough gray line on the side of the box. Nothing, then out of nowhere a red-yellow flame explodes on the end of the stick, so hot it'll burn your finger if you touch it.

"Where did you get these?" He's not yelling, but it's worse than yelling because you can hear the yelling in the quiet voice.

"I…I found them…"

"What were you doing nosing around in my closet?" His voice is as cold as a shark cruising a night sea.

"It's not like that. I was…I found the box and thought you'd… they're your medals, aren't they? You won them because you were a hero—"

"Hero?" He literally roars the word, sounding as loud and scary as the MGM lion.

Then his voice is soft again. Soft and cold and lifeless.

"Mike Hickman was a hero. Jerry Billingsly was a hero. Bob Walters and Joe…" His voice trails off. "The heroes are the men who didn't come home."

He seems to realize then that he's still holding the frame and medals in his hand.

"Stick these back in the shoebox where you found them or throw them out with the garbage—I don't care. Just get rid of them."

"But—"

"You heard me!" Daddy's "laying down the law." His way is the only way. Period, end of discussion.

Then he tosses his birthday present on the floor, and some of the medals come off and skid across the linoleum as he stomps out of the kitchen.

That was when I had the the Big Iphany, as I was picking up Daddy's medals off the floor. In church the day before, Pastor McGuiness had preached on the Prodigal Son's iphany. He'd said the word meant a "sudden moment of understanding."

Though I was on my knees on the kitchen floor instead of in a pigsty, I'd definitely had an iphany. I *understood* then. It was perfectly clear. *Daddy doesn't love me.* He hadn't loved Mama, either. Maybe he'd been pretending before he left, or maybe he'd stopped loving us while he was gone. It didn't matter which. The result was the same either way.

I was staring at the spot on the floor where he'd dumped the medals when the last of what he was saying penetrated.

"…yourself a sandwich. There's bologna and ham. And I got soup when I went into town this morning— cream of chicken and chicken noodle."

That was supper now. Or would be until I figured out how to cook. No roast or pork chops or ribs so tender the meat fell off the bone. Or fried chicken, white gravy and mashed potatoes with Mama's special ingredient. "*I always put a tablespoon of mayonnaise in the potatoes before I turn on the mixer,*" she'd whispered to me once, in that way she had of making you feel like you and she were sharing some wonderful, private secret. "*Don't tell your father. He hates mayonnaise.*"

Daddy opened the door to the freezer. "Or there's several more frozen dinners."

We might have starved to death if it hadn't been for

frozen dinners. I'd seen the first ones in a grocery store in Tennessee and talked my grandmother into trying them out. She got two of them for ninety-eight cents each. The food was on an aluminum tray—meatloaf, corn, peas, and potatoes in one and some Chinese thing called chow mien in the other. Grandma said the meat tasted like boiled Army boots. Daddy and I lived on them.

"Spencer's bringing us this year's Christmas fruit cake tonight," he said in a voice that was probably supposed to sound cheery. "Josie's going to take it out of the oven right before he leaves so it'll still be warm."

"She made cakes this year? What for? It's not Christmas if you don't have a tree."

I hadn't meant to blurt it out like that and I expected anger. Instead, my father sagged.

"What do you want from me, Bonnie?" he said. His voice sounded worn out.

"What I want, I can't have," I said.

I noticed then that he still had dark circles under his eyes even after all these months, and a permanent wrinkle stapled between his eyebrows. He was a good-looking man —*used to be* a good-looking man—with brown hair the same color as mine and eyes that had once been bright blue but now were a shade of gray that looked like ashes frozen in ice. His face had once worn smiles comfortably, but now it was all about sharp angles. Part of the reason was that he had not yet gained back all the seventy pounds he'd lost in Korea. But I suspected his face would never look soft and warm again, no matter how much he weighed.

Chapter Four

OUR FRONT DOOR faced due west. Late afternoon visitors came to us as silhouettes out of the setting sun that formed a red blob on the horizon so bright it made the world look overexposed.

I squinted into the sun, watching the silhouette of the first of tonight's "company" turn off the highway and start up the road to the house.

I'd read once that people traveled from all over the country to an island off the coast of Florida called Key West just so they could watch the sunset because it looked like the sun was sinking down into the ocean, like maybe you ought to hear a hissing sound when it hit the water. Shoot, I'd put our sunsets up against those sunsets any day! There was always dust in the air in the evening and low, flat clouds, sabers slicing open the sky as they scuttled across, late for an appointment with some storm gathering back west. The setting sun would light up the clouds and dust from behind, painting them shades of gold, red and rose—fluffy layers of turquoise and purple. Mama had painted dozens of sunsets and even *she* never got them quite right, never captured the majesty. The sun sinking down behind the flat edge of the world was way more spectacular than it could possibly be sizzling into water.

Sometimes, what came after the sunset was even more breathtaking, when storms lit the black sky with bolts of lightning like flaming arrows. Or sheet lightning torched the prairie for an instant so bright you could make out the individual pods in the heads of the yucca plants Mama had set out as a fence around our front yard—while Daddy complained that other women planted roses, but *his* wife planted weeds. And harvest moons on the prairie —oh my. Mama only ever painted one of those, the view from inside our house, out beyond the living room window with the curtains hanging down around it, over-laid with the grid of the windowpanes. The moon was big and bright and clear, like a monstrous pumpkin sitting on the prairie. It was one of those paintings Mama called whimsical and Daddy called whimseys, though. She'd inserted the three of us into the painting, cartoonish figures perched on top of the pumpkin, licking ice-cream cones.

The approaching silhouette finally resolved into a rusty old pickup and announced its presence with the beep of a horn that made the oddest sound—more like a burp of sudden laughter than a honk. Daddy said it was all rusted out inside and that was why it sounded like it did, but I liked to believe that it sounded *joyful* because it reflected the character of the man who drove it.

Spencer Daniels hopped down out of the cab as I ran down the porch steps to greet him.

"You doin' alright, Turkey Bird?" I had no idea why he'd always called me that and I'm sure he didn't, either. The nickname came out of nowhere and had no connec-tion to any person, thing or event in my life. Spencer was the Granger County postmaster and the only adult I was allowed to call by his first name.

A small round man with a neatly trimmed mustache, Spencer fairly danced on the spot when he talked. He had only a hair or two still remaining on top, though he did have what Mama called "a soap ring" of hair below it. His eyes were what got you, though, drawing you in. Little brown marbles beneath bushy eyebrows, Spencer's eyes were as bright as twin pilot lights. They *twinkled*. No really, they twinkled. Mama and I had looked at them closely lots of times and we'd agreed—they sparkled. Round and nut-brown, set deep inside a web of smile wrinkles, they were like elves' eyes—full of merriment and mischief.

I had always thought they were an odd match, Daddy and Spencer. Even as thin as he was, my father's six-foot-four-inch frame dwarfed his friend. Spencer would have had to stand on a piano stool to look Daddy in the eye. There was an economy to Daddy's movements, a big man's grace that was never more pronounced than when Spencer was hopping around him like a banty rooster.

But when the two of them were bent over some task together, branding cattle, mending a fence or playing late-night penny-ante poker, it was plain to see their outsides didn't match their insides, that their spirits meshed and complemented each other like the inner workings of a fine, gold pocket watch.

"Somebody told me there aren't gonna be any Christmas trees this year," he said, then grinned at my father, who had stepped out onto the porch behind me. "But I told them that was rubbish, that a fine, upstanding gentleman like William Beaufort McGrath the Third would rather scrub the toilet in a gas-station bathroom with a Q-Tip than disappoint his little girl."

All the fun drained out of Spencer's arrival. Spencer'd

been my grandfather's best friend, said Daddy felt like a son to him, and it was clear he believed Daddy was a good father to the precious little daughter he *loved so much*. I had never tried to tell him any different because I knew even Spencer wouldn't believe me. And I couldn't bear the thought of Spencer looking at me with sad eyes and telling me I was imagining things, or worse—taking offense that a little girl would say such a terrible thing about her own father.

"I hear they're planning a donkey barbecue here tonight and your daddy's gonna be the donkey," Spencer said as we turned toward the house. He followed me into the kitchen, pulling my ponytail and sending me into gales of giggles by tickling me in the special spot on my ribs that only he could find.

"Would you like a cup of coffee?" Daddy asked Spencer, then looked a reproachful "no" at me when I went to pour myself one, too. Mama had let me have coffee—one cup in the morning. Even doctored up with milk and sugar, I always felt all grown up when I drank it.

"Your coffee tastes like battery acid, Beau."

"Drink a lot of battery acid, do you?"

"Rosie's coffee always slid down smooth as honey."

I felt like I was going to throw up, must have looked like it, too. Spencer knew he'd stepped in it when I barreled past him toward the bathroom. I didn't heave, but it was a near thing. It was the surprise, that was all. Blind-sided. Just the thought of Mama had been enough to make me burst into tears at first, when it felt like my heart had been hacked out of my chest with a rusty tomahawk. I wasn't like that anymore, though, except when it came out of nowhere.

I ran cold water over my wrists like Mama'd shown me to do that time I had strep throat and felt like I was going to pass out every time I stood up. Then I wet a cloth and slowly washed my face. The child in the mirror who looked back at me over the sink was so pale the freckles on her face stood out like pepper on a fried egg. She was clearly an absolutely devastated human being.

"That makes two of us," I told her softly.

Two of Us. That was the name of one of Mama's horses.

She'd brought the first two walkers to Texas from her father's horse farm in Tennessee a month after we moved in. I grew up watching her tend and train the magnificent animals, tall horses with necks longer than the horses Daddy used on the ranch and small delicate ears.

Both were registered, could trace their lineage back to Black Allan, the foundation sire of the Tennessee Walking Horse breed, but Mama still had to train them in the exaggerated high steps called the Big Lick that won prizes in the show ring—make sure their rear hooves overstepped the prints of their front by at least twelve inches, preferably eighteen.

While Mama brushed their long manes and tails to make them shiny, she told me stories about famous walkers. She said the Lone Ranger's horse, Silver, had been played by a Tennessee Walking Horse, as had Roy Rogers's horse, Trigger, and she dreamed of one day training a national champion.

She had high hopes for Mr. Potato Head, the little chestnut colt we called Tater. He was one of four horses she'd reluctantly placed in the ranch foreman's care when we went to Tennessee to visit Grandma and Grampa that last time. There were also two black stallions—Aladdin and Burnt Toast and Tater's mother, a bay mare named The Two of Us. The name was some private joke between Daddy and Mama. If Daddy came into the show ring while she was working Two-sy, Mama would give him a funny little smile and tell him, "Now, if only it was just"— and they'd say the rest in unison—"the two of us." Then they'd laugh.

Daddy got rid of all Mama's horses.

I have a carrot in my pocket for Tater. I snatched it off my lunch tray at school. He loves carrots and he'll smell it on me. As soon as I step into his stall, he'll start sniffing me, butting me with his head, trying to find it.

I set my books down in the tack room and pick up the curry comb. Aladdin needs brushing. He's so tall I can't reach his back without standing on a stool, so one of the ranch hands always does that part.

"Taaaaaaater," I start calling as I cross through the breezeway from the show ring to the barn and horse stalls. "Guess what IIIII-IIII got."

The barn is unusually quiet and still. I unlatch the door to Tater's stall and open it. It's empty. That's odd. Why would one of the hands have taken Tater—where? I'd come in through the show ring and it was empty. In the wintertime, Mama only worked the horses in the show ring, where it was warm, and the temperature was hovering near zero outside.

Maybe somebody put Tater in his mother's stall with her. I go to Two-sy's stall…it's too quiet in here…and open the door. Her stall is empty, too. The curry comb drops out of my suddenly numb fingers. Fear begins to fill my belly and I rush to find Aladdin and Burnt Toast. My hands are shaking and I fumble the latches on their stall doors before I manage to fling them open. Their stalls are empty, too.

They've been stolen!

Terror grips my heart at the thought. Mama said they were worth a lot of money, but who could have taken them? Here in Texas, who would even want them?

I race out of the barn. Daddy. I have to find Daddy!

I start toward the house, then spot him down by the cattle barn, talking to the ranch foreman, Stokey.

"Daddy!" I cry as I run toward him. "Daddy, somebody took them, somebody's stolen Mama's horses!"

Stokey turns and walks away.

I crash into Daddy, breathless, babbling.

"They're gone, all four of them. I went to give Tater a carrot and—"

"I sold them," Daddy says.

I grab Daddy's arm and start dragging him back toward the barn. "You have to come and see, look. They're all gone."

Daddy pulls away from my grip on his arm and stops. "I know they're gone. I just told you. I sold them."

I try to breathe, but the air has turned as thick as creek mud. I don't even know how to think about what he's saying.

"Sold them?"

"There's no reason to keep them. They're no good to use on the ranch."

"Sold…?"

Daddy's face softens a little. "I'll get you a pony if you want something to ride."

"A pony? Aladdin and Two-sy and Tater…how could you—? A pony!"

"Out there in the barn every day, just waiting…" His voice trails off. Then his face hardens. "Like I said, there's no reason to keep them anymore."

Then he turns toward where Stokey is leaned against the side of the cattle barn, smoking a cigarette and watching us. And Daddy walks away.

Maybe that was that day I crossed the line from not loving him to hating him.

Chapter Five

When I returned to the kitchen, Spencer looked at me sympathetically and Daddy didn't look at me at all. He cut the three of us pieces of Josie's fruitcake, and I pushed mine around on my plate for a while. Daddy didn't eat much of his either. Then the other men on the association board began to arrive. Chores done, dinner eaten, they had shaved for the second time that day—and Spencer always maintained it was a poor day that demanded a man shave more than once—and gathered in our parlor to talk. Daddy sent me to bed then, though both of us knew I wouldn't be going to sleep anytime soon, and one of us knew I wouldn't even be going to bed.

As soon as I saw the last pickup truck pull up out front, I crept out of my room, down the stairs and tiptoed into the hall, where the low rumble of gruff voices and the restless shifting of worn Tony Lama boots came from behind the closed door of the parlor. I hurried back up the stairs and grabbed the scrap quilt Granny McGrath had made for me before she died, pulled it off my bed and snuggled up warm in it—well, as warm as it was possible to get lying on a cold hardwood floor with my ear to the crack under a door.

"This Christmas tree situation is serious bidness." That was Rufus Fitzsimmons, the owner of Fitzsimmons Industries that included two grain elevators and Granger County's only cotton gin. The harried little man who always had a thin sheen of sweat on his brow even when it was cold outside was more frazzled than usual because a combination of low temperatures last summer and too much rain in September meant his gin would be running twenty-four seven well into January. "It ain't like we can just trot out the back door and cut us down a tree."

I smiled. *Dufus* Fitzsimmons. Spencer always called him that, said he couldn't hit sand if he fell off a camel, and he wasted ninety percent of every conversation and half of every association meeting telling people what they already knew.

"Nobody's suggesting we cut down our own Christmas trees…Rufus," Spencer said. Did he almost say Dufus? He *did*, he almost said Dufus! I bit down hard on my lip to keep from giggling. "Nobody's suggesting anything yet, but that's why we're here—so maybe somebody can come up with a suggestion that'll work."

Clarence McMillen cleared his throat, and I sucked in a breath, hoping there might be a show. He was a blunt man, some would say harsh. Daddy liked him a lot. His ranch was just down the road. Not nearly as big as ours, he'd converted almost all of it into farmland where he grew cotton. When our cattle got out into his cotton fields, he was capable of the most colorful cursing I'd ever heard.

"I'm not gonna put lipstick on this pig," he said. "We need to be clear how we got here. We signed up to get trees this year at that new place—Santiago's ChristmasLand…

Tree Imporium…*whatever*—way up in the mountains to Sam Hill and gone because—"

"Those trees were better trees than the ones we used to get," Spencer put in, which was a cow patty served medium rare and everybody knew it. Daddy'd picked the place in the Sangre De Cristos because he'd served in Korea with the owner, one of the heroes who didn't come home.

"A Christmas tree's a Christmas tree," Mr. McMillen scoffed. "We could have gotten trees that'd do just fine at Clayton's Trees, same as last year. But you got us painted into a corner with this place Nanook of the North and a team of sled dogs couldn't find—and now we can't get any from Clayton's, either."

"I've tried, talked to those folks at Clayton's till I'm blue in the face," Frank Noakes said. "They're sold out."

Several voices spoke at once and I couldn't identify any individual ones.

"Everybody's sold out."

"We shouldn't have waited so long to—"

"Beau, you need to do *something!*"

"It's too close to Christmas to—"

"There might be a few scraggly trees left in lots up in Lubbock or Amarillo." A voice rose above the rest. "But they're so picked over they'd just be sticks." It was George Harper. I couldn't identify him for a moment because I couldn't smell him. Mr. Harper ran the drugstore, and he always smelled like he'd just spilled somebody's stinky medicine down the front of his shirt. I could almost see him slicking his hair back from his forehead like he always did when he was upset. "Fact is, everybody else already got their trees."

"Everybody but us," said Harvey Lanscombe. "I don't know about the rest of you, but there's going to be hell to pay at my house if I don't find us a tree somewhere. I'm not sure who'll scalp me first—Mildred or the kids."

"Surely, there's somewhere we could—" Dufus again.

"We're wasting time with the surely-there-must-be-somewhere crap," said Pete Prichard, a big man with a shaggy beard and bushy mustache.

Virgil Thackeray banged his cane on the floor. "Beau, *you* need to step up to the plate here and get us some trees!" Adding in what was clearly a dig at my father's military career: "A thing like this justifies *heroic measures*!"

"Apparently, there aren't any trees anywhere to get," said Jack Kavanagh, trying to be reasonable. "We're here tonight to decide what we're going to do about that."

"What *can* we do about it?" Frank Noakes wanted to know.

"Seems to me there ought to be—"

"You're like a dog worrying a bone, Rufus!" Jack Kavanagh finally lost his temper. "Give it up. Reality is this: no trees. Now what?"

The room fell silent then, and for the second time that night, I was afraid I might throw up. These men were here to ream out my father for picking the wrong Christmas tree supplier…and then *figure out how to fix the mess he'd made.* That was their job. They were the Cattlemen's Association, after all, and if they couldn't fix it, who…? It occurred to me then for the first time that maybe there was no remedy to be found, no fix, that maybe Daddy had managed to spoil Christmas for me and for everybody else in the whole county.

Then the voices started up again and droned on and on, offering up one lame plan after another, arguing this point and fist-pounding about that, rising and falling in a kind of melody.

I didn't even realize I had nodded off until I felt Daddy's big rough hand on my shoulder.

"You've been listening again," he said. "What have I told you about eavesdropping?"

I got to my feet, pulling the quilt around me for warmth. "What all those men were saying…are we really not going to have a Christmas tree? Nobody's going to have a tree?"

"Bonnie honey, we're going to celebrate Christmas just like every other year."

"Without a tree?"

He said nothing. What could he say?

I stared up at him, speechless. So many things I wanted to say were backed up in my head, jammed in there so tight I couldn't possibly get them free to say them. So much he had ruined. So much…

"I hate you," I said, brushed past him and rushed up the stairs to my room. This time, I did slam the door.

Chapter Six

DADDY SHOOK me awake just after first light. That was odd, even for a Saturday.

During the week, he always stood at the foot of the stairs and hollered up at me that he wasn't going to take me to school if I missed the bus, that I'd just have to walk. It was an empty threat and we both knew it. Richland Elementary School was in town, fourteen miles away. And anyway, I never missed the bus. I came close a few times in the beginning, trying to get the rhythm of things, timing the last possible second I could slide out from under the warm blankets and put my feet on the cold floor and still have time to get ready all by myself.

My hair was the issue. I hadn't cut it since Mama died because I wanted it to grow as long as hers had been. Now, it hung almost to my waist, and that was a lot of hair to deal with. If I could have braided it…but I didn't know how. I'd tried to figure it out once, stood in front of the bathroom mirror for a whole Saturday afternoon, and all I had to show for the effort was a scraggly length of hair that looked like a frayed rope. I decided then it wasn't possible to teach yourself to braid. So I just pulled my hair back with headbands. My favorite was decorated with the remains of the hat Grandma'd given Mama for her birthday, covered in "roses for my Rose." My grandmother's cat had shredded the hat but Mama salvaged a single black rose and attached it to my blue headband.

Daddy wanted me to cut my hair short. He didn't understand *anything!* He had cleaned out Mama's easel and painting stuff, boxed it up and stuck it in the attic. And had taken all Mama's pictures off the walls! But this was *my hair,* my last gate in the fence. Everybody knew that as long as you left the gate open, kept everything exactly the way it had been before, there was always a chance the horse would come back to the barn.

"I got something to show you," he said.

"Whatever it is, I don't want to see it." I tried to roll over to go back to sleep, but he wouldn't let me.

"Come on. You'll want to see *this.*"

Now I was curious. He motioned for me to follow as he crossed to the window seat set in the slanted wall of the attic bedroom. I danced along barefoot on the cold floor behind him as he reached out and pulled back the faded flour-sack curtains.

On a clear day, a day when the sand didn't blow or the heat rise in those wiggly lines that made it look like there was water where there really wasn't, you could see Fitzsimmons Industries' two grain elevators from my bedroom window—where they sat like toys on the horizon eleven miles away.

But this morning there were no grain elevators on the horizon. There was no horizon, only a fuzzy whiteness. Still sleepy, it was a moment before I understood.

"Snow," I whispered. I didn't say it out loud because that would have been like talking in church.

Snow was rare in west Texas. Oh, we'd get what the old folks called a blue norther a time or two every year in January or February that would deposit a few inches—sometimes a few feet—of snow. And once when I was in the first grade, they let out school and it didn't melt off for three whole days. But snow at Christmastime...it was like what you saw on the front of Christmas cards—where rosy-cheeked people all bundled up in warm coats were singing Christmas carols out in front of a house like the ones in Tennessee, where my grandparents lived. It had never in my lifetime snowed in December.

I rubbed the sleep out of my eyes and blinked, but I wasn't imagining the white fairy world that was materializing outside my window.

Daddy sat down on the window seat, so big he took up almost the whole thing. He probably intended for me to sit on his lap. I didn't, just squeezed into the small space between him and the wall and stared out the window.

The snow drifted straight down out of the pale sky, huge flakes that looked as big as the balls of cotton that dangled out of the brown plants in our fields before the Mexican farm workers pulled it out and stuffed it in long, white sacks they dragged in the dirt behind them. Whenever he could, Daddy borrowed a cotton picker from Clarence McMillen after he'd gotten his own crop in. The machine sprayed the picked cotton out a tall pipe into the high-walled cotton trailer. The snow looked like the cotton spraying out of the pipe—only slower, like it was stepping daintily out of the clouds to fall on bare ground and dead brown grass that wasn't used to such gentleness.

We sat together in silence, Daddy and I, watching the

snow change everything, transforming a world that knew so little beauty.

"Snow can even make ugly things beautiful," I whispered softly to myself.

Then the snowflakes began to swirl, caught up in the prairie wind that sent tumbleweeds bouncing across the plains, bumping into fence posts and each other, slowly coating themselves in white. Even the wind didn't seem rough and rowdy and harsh though. The snow even made it gentle somehow. It was quiet, too, didn't howl or moan, just silently spun the snowflakes, square dancers with billowing skirts that swung around and around…

Suddenly, Daddy stiffened.

"Dang!" he said. Not loud, but in the silence it echoed like he'd fired a shotgun. Clearly, that wasn't the word he was thinking. He stood up abruptly, caught me before he knocked me onto the floor, and set me back on the window seat cushion; then he was moving, long strides that carried him out the door and down the stairs, taking them two at a time.

Chapter Seven

I PADDED along behind him in my bare feet, wondering what in the world...

He didn't stop until he was standing in front of the telephone on the wall. That telephone was an extravagance Daddy made work when we first moved into the big old house by going in with three other ranchers to run a party line from town.

He noticed me for the first time then. "Go get dressed. Wear something warm."

Daddy called Spencer, but he was only the first. Daddy didn't have to convince him like he did the other men he called, though—all those who'd been at our house the night before and a whole bunch who hadn't. Mostly, he just told those men to round up their neighbors and hightail it over to our place.

I heard him say in phone call after phone call that he'd done what they'd demanded he do the night before. By the third or fourth call, he had a spiel down.

"Look, you said it was my job to get us some Christmas trees. Well, I've done what you asked. Now it's your turn.

You want trees…show up at my house this afternoon after lunch or there won't be any."

He brooked no questions, refused to explain further, and left them wondering. When he finished making calls, he sat hunkered over the kitchen table with the stub of one of my No. 2 lead pencils from school, jotting down figures and making short lists as I poured myself a bowl of Wheaties—Breakfast of Champions—and finished off the last of the pot of coffee Daddy'd made when he got up. I went upstairs and dressed and had just washed my bowl and our two cups when Spencer pulled up out front.

"I'm used to coming when called like a good hound dog," Spencer said as he sat down in a kitchen chair and pushed it back to balance on two legs. "But I did leave behind a gate I was helping Joey mend, so you might want to tell me what I'm doing here before he has cattle out all over the road and you have to help us round them up again."

Daddy had made a fresh pot of coffee, and he set a cup down in front of Spencer, then took a sip of his own. "I'll wager the day you had planned won't be nearly as entertaining as chasing tumbleweeds."

I saw Spencer's mind stumble, trying to catch the train of Daddy's thought before it pulled out of the station altogether and he had to ask for an explanation. It was a kind of unspoken game they played because they related to each other so intuitively. Knowing what the other meant without having to ask was part of the game.

"Tumbleweeds." Spencer said the word softly as he took a slow sip of coffee, stalling. If it wasn't instantaneous, it didn't count.

And then it came to him. As understanding spread across his face, his grin had to race to keep up with it.

"What a coincidence! I told my Josephine just this

morning when I left the house, 'I sure do hope I get to make a total fool of myself today!'"

"Stick with me and you'll get the chance," Daddy said.

"But why do we have to chase the little buggers? Why not just—?"

I couldn't contain myself a moment longer. I had not been a party to the instant understanding that had flashed between Daddy and Spencer. "What are you talking about?"

"It is a devious plan, my dear," Spencer said, an accent that was vaguely British coloring his west Texas twang. "It is cunning in its audacity and brilliant in its simplicity."

"I don't have any idea what you just said."

Spencer reached out to pat my head, but didn't. I loved him for that. Then he danced his black eyebrows up and down, held an imaginary cigar to the corner of his mouth and said in his best Groucho Marx voice, "It's so crazy, it just might woik—" he paused dramatically "—*if* your father has the stones to talk everybody else into it."

The two exchanged a look I couldn't read.

After that, they ignored me, deep in discussion about washtubs and baling wire. When it first began to dawn on me what they were planning, I couldn't find anywhere in my mind to put something so outlandish. Surely, they weren't planning to…But the more they talked, the more it became clear that was exactly what they were planning. I looked at Daddy and couldn't help feeling a certain admiration for the boldness of the plan that was born and drew first breath in the warmth of our kitchen—while the snow danced outside the window and swirled into little mounds against the fence posts.

Chapter Eight

BY LUNCHTIME, pickups, cattle trucks and even a mule-drawn wagon from neighboring farms and ranches and some from town filled the area in front of the house all the way to the barn. Men stood huddled together in small groups on the lee side of a few cattle trucks, battered Stetsons pulled down low over their eyes and collars turned up to the wind.

It was a testimony to the force of my father's will that so many men had actually shown up, even though Daddy never told any of them why he wanted them to come.

Rufus Fitzsimmons was there. So was George Harper, Clarence McMillen, Pete Prichard and Virgil Thackeray, along with other men who weren't on the Cattlemen's Association board. Most of them had grown up within twenty miles of where they were standing, though there was a scattering of Away-From-Here's in the crowd, people who'd moved to town to open a business maybe, or came to Granger County to take over the farm when an ailing relative died. But there weren't many of those. Muleshoe, Texas, wasn't exactly a tour-bus destination for the best and the brightest. If you didn't have a reason to be in Granger County, you left. Those who remained—whether they'd done so out of choice or necessity—formed a community that knew everybody's business and more or less looked after their own. But the very nature of the High Plains was that it attracted the independent sort, men willing to go it alone in an uninviting environment, who'd stuck it out with sheer grit, and who stood in our front yard harboring a range of emotions that began at confused and stopped by annoyed and irritated on the way to pissed off.

When Daddy stepped out on the porch, he let the spring on the screen door pull it shut with a bang that caught everyone's attention, not that he needed a bugle to announce his entrance.

He didn't have a chance to say a word.

"Where's the trees?" demanded Jerry Halburton. He was Roger Halburton's father, and it was easy to see where the boy had gotten his charm and winning personality. "I don't see no trees, and my wife and kids are gonna skin me alive if I come home without one."

"There aren't any trees…" Daddy began. A great grumble of anger and disbelief burst from the crowd like a loud burp. In the beat of silence that followed, Daddy added, "…*yet.*"

"What do you mean there ain't any trees *yet?*" Frank Noakes asked. "We got to wait for them to be delivered?"

"Or are we supposed to grab us a handful of seeds, plant them right here in the dirt and wait till they grow?" Ed Baldwin's fat lower lip turned down in an ugly sneer.

"I told you on the phone you had to do your part or there wouldn't be any trees."

"What's our part?"

"You gotta help me catch them."

That was a conversation stopper.

"And put them together."

You could have heard a gnat in house shoes tiptoeing across a cotton ball in the stillness that followed. The wind flapping a saddle blanket on the line in the back yard sounded like the applause of a one-person audience.

Daddy made a sweeping gesture out toward the prairie. "The closest thing we're gonna get to trees is right out there."

The crowd looked as one where he pointed, perhaps expecting to see pine and spuce trees mingled with the tumbleweeds blowing across the prairie.

Then George Harper figured it out. "You're not talking about...*tumbleweeds?*" he said, totally incredulous, so shocked his voice was high and reedy. "Are you?"

"That's exactly what I'm talking about."

Spencer hopped up on the porch then and took the handoff. "We got it all figured out," he said. "We dip them in washtubs full of green paint—I don't have any idea how much we'll need, but I already called around and we can lay our hands on twenty or thirty gallons right here in Muleshoe—and close around—Littlefield, Texaco, Hereford, Shallowwater. And if we have to, there's plenty to be had in Lubbock or Amarillo. Once the paint dries, we tie three tumbleweeds together with bailing wire with the biggest on the bottom—like a snowman. That way they'll stand up on their own. Won't need a tree stand."

"No," Virgil Thackeray said, "we won't need a tree stand *because a stack of tumbleweeds isn't a tree!*"

"It's a prairie tree," Spencer said. "Closest thing we got."

In a lot of ways tumbleweeds were a reflection of the cowboys who'd preceded settlers out into the Big Empty. They were homely, stickery, lanky, footloose ramblers as much a part of the canvas of everyday life as wind, sand, rattlesnakes, horned toads and tarantula spiders. We'd learned in science class that tumbleweeds started life as Russian thistles, which didn't use the wind or birds or sticker claws to spread their seeds. They just broke off at the base, and because they were shaped like a ball, they tumbled along with the wind, scattering seeds wherever they went.

"You're serious, aren't you, Beau." Clarence McMillen yanked off his hat, slammed it against his leg in frustration, and let fly a colorful stream of expletives. "I had things to do today and I wasted two hours coming over here so you could tell us we're gonna *pretend* we got Christmas trees."

A vein in Daddy's temple began to throb. "These won't be 'pretend' Christmas trees," Daddy said. "They'll be real. No, they won't look like a pine tree or a blue spruce or a cedar tree. But you can hang decorations on them same as you can a spruce tree. You can string lights around them just like a tree and drape popcorn and cranberry strings on them. You telling me your wives aren't fit to be tied because they don't have *something* to decorate?"

He turned to Harvey Lanscombe. "You said last night you were about to be scalped because there weren't any trees."

Then he looked at George Harper. "Wouldn't your Billy rather have his gifts under a tree with lights and decorations—even if it doesn't look like the one he had last year?"

To Frank Noakes, he said, "Your Emily would rather leave milk and cookies out for Santa in front of a tree, wouldn't she—no matter what it looks like."

Then he addressed the whole crowd. "My little girl has been crying herself to sleep night after night over not having a Christmas tree," he said. "I'd rather give her *something*—even if it's not perfect—than nothing at all."

I stopped breathing. Just stopped. Didn't gasp or hold my breath or anything dramatic like that. Breathing just didn't happen because I was frozen in place. Every muscle in my body turned to stone. The blood in my veins went solid; my heart stopped. Since the day my father got home, he had done nothing, not even one little thing *just for me*, just to make me happy. Then I got it and the air whooshed out of me again. I was part of the sell job. I was poster girl for the Don't You Want Your Kids to Have a Tree campaign, a prop for Daddy to use to convince people to go along with his crazy idea.

Spencer was speaking when I tuned back in. "...is how we live. We don't sit around and mope about what we don't have; we make do with what we do have. We don't have trees. We do have tumbleweeds. It doesn't get any more simple than that."

He paused then, looking deep into the baffled faces of the men in the crowd.

"Unless one of you has a better idea, that is. We can chuck this whole plan right now and go home if somebody can come up with any other way for us to get Christmas trees."

Silence. Then grumbling, but it didn't sound like before —surprised and angry. This was discussion grumbling, the beginnings of assent.

"You act like you want us to run out there and chase them tumbleweeds down right this minute," Rufus Fitzsimmons said. It was the first discernible move from should we do this to *how* should we do this? "Why'd you drag us all out here like your pants were on fire. It's not like we're suddenly gonna run out of tumbleweeds."

"We *will* run out of tumbleweeds *we can use* unless we get them today—right now," Daddy said. "With this snow, they'll get caught up against the fences in drifts—wet and smashed and useless. We have to have the ones that are still round."

Then Daddy went on like there'd been a vote and he'd won. "We're going to have to be smart about this," he said. "We only have a few hours until sundown, and if this snow gets worse, we won't even have that long. We have to gather up as many weeds as we can and let them dry overnight. Then we can paint them in the morning."

"Dry? Don't you mean *freeze?*" Ed Baldwin said. "Or didn't you notice that *it's snowing?* And all that green paint, it's gonna freeze, too."

"Not in my show barn it won't," Daddy said.

There was a beat of silence. They'd all heard about it, but there were some who thought it was as much a myth as the Lone Ranger.

"You mean that thing really is *heated?*"

Daddy continued as if he hadn't heard. "We'll assemble them tomorrow night, and you can take one home with you when you leave. Whatever's left, we'll hand out free to anybody who shows up looking for a tree—right up until Christmas Eve."

And then he became the Marine who'd won all those medals he wouldn't let me display in a frame, singling out first one person and then another for specific jobs, never once asking if they were willing to cooperate, just telling them what to do. George Harper was to be in charge of getting the baling wire to tie the tumbleweeds together. How much? Just get a lot of it, Daddy said. Roberto Ortega was to come up with washtubs. He immediately pulled out a scrap of paper from his pocket and started cornering the men who were dispersing, jotting down who could bring a washtub when they came back to paint the trees tomorrow morning. Frank Noakes was assigned to hook up our high-walled cotton trailer to his pickup and bring it along to put the tumbleweeds in.

Pete Prichard was put in charge of rounding up the green paint. He was to clean out Muleshoe Mercantile and Rowden's Five and Dime before he branched out to the surrounding communities.

"That much paint'll cost…" Mr. Prichard thoughtfully stroked his beard that hung down the front of his shirt. "How'm I gonna pay for it?"

"My plan, my nickel," Daddy said.

"How much paint should I get?"

"I don't know." Daddy shrugged. "All of it, I guess."

Chapter Nine

DADDY and I rode with Spencer in his rattly-bang old pickup. I sat in the middle, where chunks of cotton and springs stuck out through a hole in the old leather seat. He and Spencer had talked about where would be the best spot—the most wide-open piece of land with no fences anywhere near—and had concluded that south of our cotton field would be as good a spot as any.

The wind had picked up as we led a ragtag caravan of pickups and cattle trucks down the dirt road to the end of the field and then out across the prairie beyond it. The snow was still coming down, not heavy snow, just a constant white all around us like looking at the world through gauze.

Spencer pulled up a mile or so past the cotton field, and he and Daddy got out and walked out away from the truck. The other trucks stopped, too, and men climbed down out of them and joined Daddy and Spencer. I stayed behind, watching a scene that appeared and disappeared in rhythm with the wipers' scraping course across the windshield.

It was only then that it was clear a lot of the men who'd been standing in front of our house a few minutes ago had gotten in their trucks when Daddy was done talking alright—and gone home. But I was impressed with how many had stayed. It was a foundational life lesson in the power of desperation. Some of them were men I wouldn't have expected to sign on to such a harebrained idea.

Frank Noakes got down out of his pickup. He owned the dry cleaner's in town, a fastidious little man I'd never seen without a crease in his pants.

Jack Kavanaugh was the principal of the high school. He was a stern, no-nonsense man with a limp he'd gotten when a land mine blew off his left leg from the knee down in the Battle of the Bulge.

Roberto Ortega and Jose Vasquez were Mexicans who'd been babbling to each other in Spanish, a sound like crackling flames, the whole time Daddy was talking. It hadn't seemed to me like they were agreeing with him, but it's hard to tell which way a man's leaning when you can't understand a word he says.

Pete Prichard was no surprise. He had nine children and he'd probably have done anything up to and perhaps including cutting off his own arm to see that they all had a good Christmas.

Charlie Bracewell was no surprise, either. He'd been watching Daddy with a kind of tautness in him like a bowstring with the arrow ready to fly, his deeply lined bloodhound face a study in concentration. He had served with Patton in North Africa during the war.

It was also interesting to note who had gone home. Harvey Luscombe apparently decided he'd rather be scalped, and Jerry Halburton preferred to be skinned alive than be a party to this grand scheme. Clarence McMillen, who'd yelled the loudest at the meeting, was nowhere to be seen. Neither was Virgil Thackeray, who'd pointed out that the mess was Daddy's fault and it was his job to fix it even if he had to use heroic measures. Mr. Thackeray must not have been feeling very brave this afternoon.

The men gathered in a semicircle around Daddy, awaiting orders. It was his good fortune that a bouncing tumbleweed hit him in the back as he was about to speak. He grabbed it and held it out like you'd hold up a twenty-pound trout.

"Round," he said, "like this one."

And without another word, he headed over to the cotton trailer to deposit his prize. The other men stood looking at each other, not quite sure how to proceed; then Frank Noakes took aim on a tumbleweed that was bouncing by about fifteen feet away and took off after it. The others followed suit.

It didn't take long to figure out that catching tumbleweeds on the run was going to be harder than it'd sounded listening to Daddy talk about it on our porch. For starters, nobody'd counted on not being able to catch up with the bouncing weeds, though it was hardly an even match. The tumbleweeds were being propelled across the prairie by a gusty wind that kept them constantly moving. And they quickly bounced out of the grasp of the men chasing them —because the men were doing well just to stand up. That was another problem Daddy hadn't foreseen. The ground was bone dry and hard as an anvil. With the thin layer of snow on top, the prairie had become as slick as a giant frozen pond.

Rufus Fitzsimmons was the first to go down, sprawling on his backside and sliding like a kid coming in to home plate. He tripped George Harper, who had just about laid hands on a lone tumbleweed, and the two of them became a tangle of boots, hats and flailing arms. Jose Vasquez was running after a weed, a hopeless race, and as it pulled away from him, he made a desperate dive for it, coming up short and sliding forward on his belly. If he'd landed on it, the weed would have been useless anyway. Charlie Bracewell did smash one—lost his footing and fell on it. He stood up holding a shapeless form of broken sticks.

While the others slipped and slid and fell all over themselves on the glassy prairie, Daddy and Spencer held a hasty war conference next to the tailgate of Rufus Fitzsimmon's cattle truck—a conference punctuated by elaborate hand motions on Spencer's part and a look of rapt attention on Daddy's. Then Daddy grabbed Frank Noakes, spoke into his ear, and Frank leapt into his truck and headed back to our barn.

Before the others could get their wits about them long enough for the grand plan to fall apart on the spot, Daddy hollered out above the wind what was rapidly becoming obvious to everybody.

"This isn't going to work," he said. "We gotta try something else."

"The trucks can get traction through the snow," Spencer called out, "and they can keep up with these little varmints. Double up and we'll use the pickups. Put two men in the back of each. One'll have a pitchfork, a hoe, a rake, a stick—anything to spear them with. If you need something, Beau just sent Frank back to the barn." He gestured toward our house, where the truck had already appeared coming back.

"Think of it like you was roping a calf," Spencer said. "Pick you out a tumbleweed, come up alongside it and scoop it up into the bed of the truck. The second man can hang onto the ones you catch until you have a load to take to the cotton trailer."

"Come on, men," Daddy called out. There was life in my father's voice like I hadn't heard in a long time. "Let's run 'em down."

And then began what I would later recall as the Mad Tumbleweed Chase.

Chapter Ten

DAD CROUCHED low in the back of Spencer's old pickup just behind the cab. One hand gripped the cold metal of the back siding, and the fingers of the other were wound tight around the handle of an old pitchfork with two broken tines that'd been in the bed of the truck. I would be the hold-onto-the-weed member of the crew, but stayed in the cab where it was warm until we caught something for me to hang onto.

Spencer slid in behind the wheel, sending a shower of snowflakes off his sleeve. He banged the pickup door shut twice before it caught.

"Hold on real tight," he said. "Get a feel for how rough it's going to be when you're out there in the truck bed... because this isn't going to be a sled ride."

The prairie looked flat and empty from a distance. But close up, it was not the smooth surface it appeared to be. Russian thistles that had yet to die and become migratory tumbleweeds were everywhere, interspersed with yucca plants, clumps of buffalo grass and half a dozen other grasses I didn't know the names of, alongside sand sage and small, what I called "hand cactus." All of that grew out of a surface of hard dirt pockmarked with a maze of prairie dog holes.

The whine of protesting gears filled the cab, and there was a breathless instant while the back tires shot snow out behind us. Suddenly, they grabbed hard ground beneath the snow and the pickup truck lurched forward. In another instant, we were flying out across the white prairie.

I cranked down the window so I could scan the prairie for a likely catch. Tumbleweeds came in all shapes and sizes. Some were as small as bowling balls; others were the size of washing machines. There were even monster weeds as big as a golf cart. Given that the plan was to stack the weeds three high in graduated sizes, we'd be able to use anything we could catch and spear. But in my mind, it had become a tumbleweed safari, and I was looking to bag the biggest prey I could find.

And there it was, a tumbleweed Daddy and Spencer together couldn't have gotten their arms around, bouncing away from us to the right. The weed came within inches of getting nailed broadside by George Harper, in hot pursuit of his own prey. He was driving his old cattle truck, with Pete Prichard clinging to the railing, leaning out with a hoe, his long beard flapping in the wind.

I grabbed Spencer's arm and pointed to the big weed. "Over there!"

Spencer nodded. "A prime specimen of tumbleweed-dom if ever I saw one."

He tapped on the back glass and made elaborate pointing motions to Daddy. Then he headed the little pickup truck in the direction the weed was bouncing, holding firm to the steering wheel as we plowed through stands of buffalo grass, smashed into Russian thistles, jolted up over yucca plants and smashed down into prairie dog holes. Jackrabbits bounded away from us, their donkey ears turning like radar dishes on their heads.

The sound of mangled cactus scraping the underbelly of the truck set my teeth on edge, and the air began to fill with a fine haze of dust that had settled through decades of sandstorms in every nook and crack of the old cab.

And then the tumbleweed was bouncing along right beside my window. I saw the pitchfork swoop down and spear it off the ground and up over the top of the cab. By the time I turned around to look out the back glass, Daddy had the tumbleweed securely in his hands in the back of the truck.

Spencer slid to a stop, and I hopped out and clambered into the truck bed. Daddy turned the weed over and handed it to me stem first—so I could hold onto the stub, away from the stickery limbs. Up close, tumbleweeds were not attractive creatures. They didn't have thorns like a rosebush, but the dry limbs were scratchy, brittle and rough.

"Sit down," Daddy said, "so Spencer doesn't launch you out over the tailgate."

I sat, but he clutched a handful of my coat sleeve, anyway. I held onto our prize weed with one hand and the side of the pickup truck with the other as Spencer took off after another prey.

Wind and snow lashed my face, whipping my ponytail into my eyes until I jammed the end of it down into the back of my coat. I got up onto my knees so I could see better around Daddy, who had his feet spread out broad for stability. A couple of times, I bounced up off the bed of the truck and dangled momentarily from Daddy's grip on my coat sleeve.

The tumbleweed Spencer was chasing was small, very dense and perfectly round, and a wily creature. Just as

Spencer was about to pull up beside it, the weed collided with a yucca plant and veered off in another direction. Spencer changed course, and when he did, he clunked down into a deep prairie dog hole. The impact launched me into the air, breaking my grip on the side of the truck. I might actually have been tossed out altogether if Daddy hadn't been holding onto me.

"Hang on!" he said. "Or you're going to be bouncing across the prairie with the tumbleweeds and we'll have to run *you* down."

"And stick me with that?" I pointed to his pitchfork and giggled.

"Yup," he said. "Right through your belly button!"

There was a light in his eyes I hadn't seen since…well, since… The lines on his face had softened, especially the ones around his mouth that pulled the corners down into a perpetual frown. He was smiling.

I found myself smiling back.

"I bet we've got the biggest tumbleweed out here," I told him.

"Now, Bonnie Leigh McGrath, this is not a contest." His face was solemn, his tone stern. But the look in his eyes didn't match. "We're not trying to see who can bag the biggest." Then the smile leapt back where it had been and snuggled in comfortably. "But ours is definitely bigger than anybody else's." He leaned close and spoke into my ear. "You keep your eyes peeled for the big ones."

It soon became clear that a competitive spirit had been carried from truck to truck with the prairie wind. Testosterone was running high and free out there on the prairie that day. No, it wasn't a contest to see who could catch the biggest tumbleweed. But yeah, it was, too.

When Spencer finally pulled up alongside our small-but-round weed, Daddy speared it easily and in one motion lifted it over the side of the truck to me. I didn't take it in my hand. I was rapidly running out of hands. I just used the big weed I already had to hold the smaller one up against the cab of the truck.

The rest of the day blended into a smeared image of wildly dancing tumbleweeds; racing, sliding trucks; and scared-up jackrabbits exploding out of the brush. The snow let off, filtering lightly out of the cloud canopy above our heads, worn thin but nowhere threadbare enough to reveal blue sky. The horizon-to-horizon prairie became crisscrossed with twin brown tracks on the white surface.

The light never changed as the sun moved across the sky behind the endless gray overcast. Time came unhooked from the world, dangling in a forever-moment of wild wrangler whoops muted by the distance, the gunning whine of straining engines and punctuated by jolts and bumps and dry yucca pods exploding over the front bumper.

I hadn't noticed the afternoon go by or evening set in. It just became increasingly dim and progressively harder to spot the tumbleweeds in a gloom that was as obliterating as the white gauzy haze of snow had been. The chase was about to be over.

Suddenly, I spotted twin streaks of light in the gloom. George Harper had turned on his headlights. Then Spencer turned on his headlights—headlight. The left one had been nailed by a particularly vicious yucca plant. One after another the truck drivers switched on lights so they could see in the growing dark and went right on chasing tumbleweeds. It became a light show then. All around, near and in the distance, twin beams of jiggling light illuminated the prairie, lighting up the pale gray-green sage and casting out harsh dagger shadows behind the sharp-edged yucca leaves. When tumbleweeds bounced in and out of the beams, the twin lights turned to follow them like a dog after a slab of beef.

When Spencer stopped briefly so Daddy and I could adjust the pile of weeds I was corralling in the back of the truck, I spotted eye-shine in the gloom.

"Daddy, look. A coyote."

The animal was just out of the light so you could see nothing more than a vague dog-shaped shadow, but it stood perfectly still, watching. Daddy and I stood still, too. Then another dark shape came up beside the first, its eye-shine reflecting the light.

"Two of them," I whispered.

Daddy didn't move, didn't even blink. He must not have heard me.

"Do you see the other—"

"Coyotes mate for life," Daddy said in a soft voice.

When we loaded our last catch of weeds into the cotton trailer, we did so by the glow of our lone headlight beam. Full night touched my neck with cold fingers and I shivered, looking up at an overcast sky that had begun to clear, revealing stars as big and bright as chunks of ice.

Our load filled the cotton trailer, and we followed Mr. Noakes as he pulled it slowly across the prairie and down the road. When I stepped into our barn, I was dumfounded. It was completely full of tumbleweeds, the pile stretching all the way to the rafters.

"Think we got enough?" Spencer asked. The other men had gone home, one after another, as they dropped off their final loads, and the three of us stood alone in the barn.

"How many do you think we'll need?"

"I don't know."

Daddy shrugged. "Neither do I."

Chapter Eleven

D~ADDY~ AND S~PENCER~ ~KEPT~ ~TALKING~, but I left them in the barn and headed into the house, peeling off my coat in a rush to hang on the hook by the back door. I couldn't wait to take a bath in the big clawfoot bathtub in the downstairs bathroom.

Daddy had told me to wear gloves, but I'd only been able to find the left one, so my right hand was scratched up like I'd lost a fight with a cougar. And the scratches itched. I'd been clawing at them all day, and the red marks had become red welts I couldn't wait to soak in hot water.

As I danced from bare foot to bare foot on the cold linoleum floor in the bathroom, shivering while the growing pool of hot water steamed the mirror over the sink, I planned out what I had to do tomorrow, ticking off the items one by one in my head.

First, coffee! I needed lots of coffee and lots of cups. We'd start early in the morning, just after first light, and the men would need it. Cups were no problem. We had Mama's whole china set. Coffee was another thing altogether, though. Daddy and I used an old percolator that would only make a few cups, but somewhere in the garage was a big one we'd used for the riders who came to compete in the show barn. I had no idea where it was or how to operate it.

Second, I had to gather up some old clothes I could paint in. I wasn't entirely sure Daddy was going to let me help with the tree painting, but even if he didn't, there'd be green paint all over everywhere and I would surely get some on whatever I wore.

And gloves. I had to find the mate to the one I wore today. No, mittens! I had an old pair stuck somewhere in a dresser drawer. I could use them, if they still fit, and then throw them away after—

I stopped, pulled up short. My mind unhooked from that thought and left it standing alone on the track, and the other thoughts slammed into the back of it like train cars smashing into a stalled engine. Then the whole line of them teetered and fell over on its side, derailed.

I'd been *excited*.

I'd been *looking forward to* doing something with Daddy!

How could that possibly be? I felt...guilty...like I'd done something bad. And I had. I had betrayed...what? My mother? No, not my mother. It took me a moment to work it all out in my head, to figure out that what I had betrayed was my own anger, my own resentment. They formed my suit of armor, and without them wrapped snug around me, I was as helpless as I'd been Back When I Cared.

I summoned my anger then, called it to me like a faithful dog. It came running, loping past the nights I'd tried to carry on a normal conversation at dinner like normal people did in normal homes were there wasn't a mute troll seated at the head of the table.

Past the first day of school when Daddy dropped me

off at the door! Never learned my teacher's name or when school let out for holidays, or that I needed a costume for the Halloween party.

Past all those goodnight kisses.

My just-washed hair is clean. Mama makes sure by pinching a strand of it and pulling it between her fingers to see if it squeaks. I step out of the damp towel Mama has wrapped around me into the pink baby-doll pajamas with lace around the neck that Grandma made for me out of fabric she let me pick out at the store.

I have brushed my teeth, too, and Mama inspects them to be certain I did a good job since it's harder to brush now without scratching the gums where the teeth are missing in front. Then Mama tells me, "Go kiss your daddy goodnight."

I race across the room and leap into Daddy's arms. He lifts me up in the air, then sets me in his lap and kisses my whole face—my nose, my cheeks, down around my neck where it tickles—and I giggle and try to squirm away, but I'm not really trying. The stubble of his beard against my face feels scratchy, but I don't care.

Then he hugs me. Really tight. Almost so tight I can't breathe. And he doesn't let me go, just holds me with his arms wrapped around me, and he snuggles down next to my ear and whispers, "I love you, Bonnie Leigh," and I whisper back, "I love you, too, Daddy."

I had yearned for that every night Daddy was gone. Even when the months became years, I never forgot, never got into bed a single night that I didn't wish my daddy had been there to kiss me goodnight. And Back When I Cared, I tried...

I'd get ready for bed—bath taken, hair washed, teeth brushed—and cross the living room to where Daddy sat cloaked by the evening newspaper he didn't even seem to be reading. It felt like a death march, the last steps to an execution, or walking the plank. Daddy always smelled like old sweat and the manure on his boots. And I'd lean over and leave a little peck on his cheek. He never acknowledged that he'd seen me.

I'd stopped kissing him goodnight the day of the Big Iphany. He didn't notice.

It was cold in my pajamas and bare feet when I left the bathroom and headed to the kitchen to make us "dinner." I was thinking a fried chicken "popsicle meal," as Spencer called them. But it appeared Daddy'd already fired up his own because I could smell the meatloaf when I entered.

Daddy was sitting at the kitchen table, drinking coffee and staring out the window. In the spill of light into the darkness you could see that it'd started snowing again.

He looked up when I came in.

"We had fun out there today, didn't we?" he said.

"It was okay," I said. I turned my back to him, went to the refrigerator and selected the beef stew dinner from the freezer.

Chapter Twelve

THE NEXT MORNING, Roberto Ortega showed up with a truckload of washtubs as Daddy and I sat finishing our coffee.

Daddy got up wordlessly, put his coat on, and went outside to help him unload the tubs in the barn. I had wanted to ask if I could help with the painting, but plunging words into his stoney silence was like sticking an ice pick in a glacier.

Instead, I went upstairs and dressed in clothes that were way too ratty for the clothes bin at church. I finally located the missing mittens—the left was in my underwear drawer and the right was under my bed. Other trucks had arrived while I was dressing, all the men who'd helped us catch last night what we were about to paint green today. They'd brought along a handful of others to help out—ranchers Harry Malone, Damien Duncan and Ernie Phelps—along with Billy Hennessy, a senior at Muleshoe High School who worked part time as a mechanic at Charlie Bracewell's Texaco Station.

I went through our barn—where one whole end was

now occupied by a mountain of tumbleweeds and through the breezeway to the show ring. I could feel the warm air escaping through the double doors that stood open wide enough to allow the men who were working to go back and forth between it and the barn. Daddy must have turned the heat on before he went to bed last night because it took a while for the fans to circulate warmth from the propane heaters at each end. The ring had stood cold and empty, the rows of stadium seats gathering dust, since the last show there two years ago.

The festive atmosphere of yesterday's tumbleweed chase was gone. I suspected that overnight each man had been summoned by his own high court of common sense and interrogated about the reasonableness, or lack thereof, of bringing weeds painted green into their homes and pretending they were Christmas trees. But they'd signed on for this by participating yesterday, and these were the sort of men who'd ride whatever horse they were on all the way to the barn.

Spencer was there, of course. He paused in his conversation with Daddy long enough to wink at me. Daddy was directing the efforts of Charlie Bracewell and Billy Hennessy to position washtubs on the floor on the far end of the ring as Pete Prichard, George Harper and Rufus Fitzsimmons hauled in buckets of green paint.

Billy walked away with a tub in tow as I approached Spencer and Daddy.

"You planning on helping us paint tumbleweeds today?" Daddy asked. It sounded a little like his we-had-fun-didn't-we question last night.

I intended an emotionless response, in a pass-the-salt tone of voice that wouldn't give the slightest hint how desperately I wanted to.

"I've got on painting clothes, don't I?"

I knew the words were a mistake the moment they left my mouth. In striving for impassive and indifferent, I'd gone too far, slipped over the edge into rude. I'd never talked back to my father in my life.

I couldn't believe I'd said it until the words hung out there in the air between us like a dead rattlesnake on the end of a hoe. I watched my father's face turn to granite.

"Get smart with me, young lady, and this train leaves without you on it." His voice was dark and cold. "Get back to the house."

Spencer looked at me sympathetically as I turned and left the ring—didn't run out like a little kid about to cry, though I felt like one. I'd spoiled everything with my big mouth. I wanted desperately to be a part of all that was happening. There'd been more life in my life in the past twenty-four hours than in all the cold dark months since Mama died. And *I* had ruined it.

Hard as I tried, I couldn't blame Daddy this time, though. This one was on me.

I left the show ring, but I was determined not to miss what was going on in there. I went around to the back of the building and slipped in through the door of the tack room that opened on the horse stalls just outside the ring. Then I sneaked carefully into the ring, climbed to the highest row of seats at the far end, crouched down behind them and made my way back to where the men were work-ing. I settled in on the floor there for a balcony view of the show below.

It was clear Daddy'd thought this through and had a plan. After the washtubs were placed strategically in the area near the door leading to the breezeway into the barn, he called on the three-man teams from yesterday, only this time one of them would select a weed out of the pile in the barn, one of them would dunk it in green paint and the third would hang it from the "clotheslines" of baling wire George Harper had strung at the other end of the ring. Each tumbleweed would be clipped to a wire with a clothespin and left there to drip green gobs of goo onto the dirt until it dried.

Daddy shrugged. The temperature outside had yet to warm up past freezing, but it was rising. That was what usually happened. A dusting of snow when the temperature dropped below 32 degrees, then the dusting would melt off the next day. In January and February, the temperature routinely plunged to minus five and six degrees, though. If it snowed then, the snow stayed around long enough to make a snowman.

Daddy's plan was sound, but just like yesterday, it needed adjusting and retooling along the way. I was sure he wasn't surprised. I once heard him tell Spencer that "no battle plan ever survives the first contact with the enemy."

The first problem became apparent quick. Most of the weeds were too big to fit into a washtub. You couldn't just dunk them. You had to roll them around and around in the paint to get all the parts covered. And that quickly became a bottleneck in the assembly line. Some of the weeds were so large, in fact, that you couldn't stuff any part of them into a tub. The first really big one was the one Daddy and Spencer and I had caught, I was sure of it, and there was nothing big enough to submerge it in. Daddy dragged out an old horse trough, and it proved to be a much better vessel to use than the washtubs, anyway—on weeds of any size. Just lay them on their sides and rotate them slowly through the trough/vat of paint.

But the biggest of the weeds, our prize included, wouldn't even fit in the trough. A spin through it left the outside edges of the weed green and all the internal limbs dry. So the bigger weeds required a second step in the painting process. Someone had to use a soup ladle out of our kitchen to scoop up paint and drip it through to the inside limbs.

Then there was the paint. Pete Prichard took considerable ribbing about the variation in colors. One was quickly dubbed baby-puke green. And there was John Deere green and stomped-bug green and pond-slime green. There were several other shades and hues, too, but the words the men used to describe them were words I didn't know. When Harry Malone said the first one, everybody laughed, so I knew it was a word I wasn't supposed to hear.

As the painting went on, the jovial atmosphere from yesterday began to return. With wisecracks and references I didn't understand, the men teased each other and made fun of the "trees." George Harper suggested Pete Prichard paint his beard green, string lights around it and stuff a candy cane in his mouth--then he wouldn't need a tree. Frank Noakes tripped and spilled half a can of baby-puke green paint in Jack Kavanaugh's lap as he sat on an upturned nail keg, slowly spinning a big tumbleweed in the horse trough. The paint ran out of his lap, down his pant legs, and into his *left* boot. The men laughed at the look on his face, but laughed even harder when Mr. Kavanagh removed his prosthetic leg, pulled the boot off it—then stood up on one foot and splashed the contents of the boot down the front of Mr. Noakes's shirt.

Chapter Thirteen

As soon as the men got near the last of the weeds in the pile, I slipped back out of the show ring and headed toward the house so I could be there when Daddy came out, like I'd been dutifully in the kitchen the whole time.

When I rounded the corner of the barn, I saw Spencer sitting on the porch, whittling the dry stalk of a yucca plant. I had a collection of Spencer's whittled stalks, probably a dozen of them. They weren't particularly artistic. Yucca stalks didn't lend themselves to creating fine details. Spencer said he whittled "for the same reason an old woman knits"—to occupy his hands. One of the stalks he'd given me—my favorite—was a claw. He said it was a chicken's foot, but I decided it was an eagle's talon. From the progress he'd made on this stalk, it was clear he'd been at it awhile. He looked up when he saw me, and I suspected he'd been waiting for me.

I plopped down dejectedly on the porch beside him. No sense trying to hide anything from Spencer. I had learned long ago that he had a creepy ability to know what I was thinking.

"Whatcha making?" I asked.

"It was an anchor until I broke a piece off, so now it's a fishhook, and I'm going to pretend that's what I intended it to be all along."

I smiled a little.

"Aha," he said. "I knew if I dug around in there deep enough, I'd find a smile hidden somewhere in your belly. Haven't seen a lot of those lately."

"What's to smile about?"

At that moment, the men began to emerge from the barn, so splattered with green paint they looked like they all had measles made of pickles. When he saw the green paint on the shirt of the fastidious Mr. Noakes, Spencer burst into a peal of contagious laughter that even made me chuckle.

Daddy came out then and stood by the barn door, talking to Mr. Fitzsimmons.

"You ever notice this?" Spencer asked, and held up his right thumb.

"That it doesn't have a nail, you mean? Yeah. What happened to it?"

"You wasn't no bigger than a fart in a whirlwind and I come over here to help your daddy build that show barn for your mama. He worked on it for months, built most of it all by himself—and he sure didn't have any use for them Tennessee Walking Horses she was gonna train in it!"

Most of the Texans I knew felt the same as Daddy did, that it was a colossal waste of time trying to teach horses to prance when they should have been out working cattle, which was what God had created them for! Mama didn't get mad at them about it, though. She just smiled and said it wasn't any more a colossal waste of time than trying not to get thrown off a bucking bull, which was *not* what God had created Brahma bulls for.

"Didn't matter that he thought it was foolishness, though," Spencer said. "Long's your mama wanted it, your daddy would have crawled over six miles of broken Coke-Cola bottles to get it for her."

I felt a funny twitching down deep in my belly.

"So I came over here when I could to help him with it, and that's when I got this." He wiggled his thumb. "Smashed it with a sledgehammer."

I cringed at the mental image. "That must have hurt!"

"Oh, it did at the time!" He whistled softly. "Whoooeeee, how it did for a fact! But then it went numb, couldn't feel a thing. See, God made us that way, fixed it so our bodies would protect us from feeling some of the things that hurt so bad you can't hardly stand the pain."

He used his nailless thumb to hold onto the yucca stalk's broad end while he worked to sharpen the other end into the fishhook he was pretending he'd intended to make.

"He made our hearts that way, too," Spencer said. "When you get hit hard with something so painful you can't stand it, you just go numb. Don't feel anything."

He held the stick out and inspected it, then went back to carving. He kept talking, but softer then.

"Where your daddy was in Korea…it was a bad place. He did some brave things, saved the lives of a whole bunch of American soldiers, but what he did got him captured by the enemy."

He glanced over at me. "You're old enough now to understand that your daddy was a—"

"POW," I said. Spencer looked surprised. "Mama told me."

Mama had gotten a phone call one morning and burst into tears. Then she'd raced out to the barn, saddled up Toastie and galloped away across the prairie. She stayed gone all day. When I finally saw her silhouette against the setting sun, I waited for her on the top step of the porch. Mama wasn't crying anymore. She got down and handed Toastie's reins to one of the ranch hands, climbed the porch steps and sat down beside me. When I asked her what was wrong, she started not to tell me, then changed her mind.

She didn't look at me when she talked. I think if I'd gotten up and walked away, she'd have kept talking anyway. She'd said she was telling me because she wanted me to hear it from her. But I think she was telling me because she needed to hear it herself to make it real.

"Did she tell you what that meant?"

I shook my head. "Just that it was bad."

"POW means prisoner of war. Your daddy spent nineteen months as a captive of the North Korean Army."

"They put him in jail?"

"Not exactly. They put him with other American soldiers—there were about seven thousand of them in the beginning, I think—in POW camps. From what I understand, he was in several different camps, every one of them worse than the last. Almost half of the American soldiers there died."

The real heroes didn't come home.

"The soldiers who survived—it was really *hard* for them. To stay alive, they had to find somewhere inside themselves they could go, a deep place to escape the real world when it was just too terrible there. I think your daddy was pretty good at checking out, probably better than most at going numb."

He held up his hand. "It took a long, long time for all the feeling to come back into this thumb after that sledgehammer got it." He smiled. "I still got a thumb, though, and it works, and I thank the good Lord for that." He wiggled the thumb up and down in front of my face. "But the nail went black and fell off, and it never grew back. My thumb isn't the same now as it was before I smashed it."

He glanced across the yard to where Daddy stood talking to Mr. Fitzsimmons.

"It won't never be the same again."

Then he bent over his fishhook and kept whittling.

Chapter Fourteen

AFTER THE MEN left and Daddy came into the house to clean up, I made sandwiches for our lunch and put them on the table. We ate in silence. Whatever sliver of light I imagined I'd seen shining out through a crack in his soul yesterday was gone now. After lunch, Daddy went back out to do the chores he'd had to set aside to concentrate on the grand tumbleweed plan.

I cleaned up what few dishes there were and went up to my bedroom and shut the door. Then I lifted the bedspread on the iron bed and felt around beneath it for the long flat box. It was dusty. Not house dust, colored dust, and there were smudges of color that came off on my fingers when I opened the lid.

The pastel crayons lay in separated rows on the cotton that lined the inside of the box. Broken pieces of crimson and azure, rubbed down to a point, rested on a carpet of fine red and blue dust.

They were my mother's pastels, an old box she'd given me to use. She'd sit for hours in her studio, teaching me how to mix and blend the chalky colors into the yellow and pink of a sunset or the angry greenish purple of a tornado cloud.

I wasn't working on anything as magnificent as the pictures that hung in gilt frames in my grandparents' house in Tennessee, pictures my mother had spent her youth creating, bent over an easel in the screened-in back porch, humming hymns in the afternoon light. Grandma had kept every picture my mother had ever painted, starting with crayon drawings when she was in the first grade. A walk through my grandparents' house was a walk through the gradual maturing of my mother's talent. There were horse pictures, of course! They were among the first, and the most crude—some of them. But a magnificent picture of Granddaddy's prize Tennessee Walker, Prancing Jack, hung above the mantel.

Mama went to boarding school for a year in New Orleans to study art, and her paintings from that time were of white-pillared mansions, green lawns and stately trees covered with gray Spanish moss, riverboats paddling up a wide, muddy river, narrow streets with wrought-iron gates and flowered balconies.

Apparently, the whimsical phase of Mama's art career began the day she met the striking young soldier who happened by her art show and stopped—probably more to look at my mother than at her paintings. The whirlwind courtship that followed didn't leave much time for the detailed landscapes she usually painted. But Mama couldn't go more than a couple of days without creating something. So she'd done a quick pastel of a woman's hand holding a giant teapot. Only a part of a woman's arm is visible and the sleeve of her red dress. Then Mama had placed herself and Daddy *inside the teapot*. She is wearing a red dress, too, and pouring Daddy a cup of tea…and sitting inside the teapot she's holding is another woman in a red dress, pouring a cup of tea for another soldier…and inside that teapot is another…

Mama brought her whimseys with her to Texas and produced more in the years she lived on the plains. You could watch me grow up in those paintings.

There's a three-year-old little girl on the saddle in front of Mama as she and Daddy ride a pair of jackrabbits across the prairie.

She and Daddy lead a longhorn bull on a leash toward a nursery school as a little girl with a lunch box swings on one of the horns.

The three of us—Mama, Daddy and a gap-toothed little girl—ride the sail of a windmill like it's a Ferris wheel.

Those paintings once hung all over the house. But when my grandparents brought me home from Tennessee, the paintings and every other trace of my mother's art were gone. I heard Grandma ask Daddy what had happened to them, and he'd said he "couldn't look at them right now." I found them later leaned against the wall in an empty horse stall in the barn. Mama's art supplies—paint, brushes, and pastel crayons and her easel and pallet were stored away in boxes in the attic. Her studio was an empty room where my shoes made a hollow echoing sound on the hardwood floor.

But Daddy didn't erase it all, couldn't remove all trace of my mother from that room! If you got down on your hands and knees and looked closely at the floor, all the cracks between the boards are filled with colored dust.

I didn't work on my own art in Mama's studio, just spread the canvasses out on the floor of my bedroom. I had a couple of works in progress. I'd just about given up on the one of the coyote because it looked like his head was on backwards and I didn't have Mama to tell me how to fix it. And I'd left the tumbleweed picture half finished, a bowling ball with bristles. The picture I was working on now was a simple one. A windmill and a blue sky. Some yucca plants and maybe a jackrabbit if I could get the ears right. It was my Christmas present for Spencer.

Chapter Fifteen

I HAD JUST ABOUT GOTTEN one ear on the jackrabbit complete when I heard the phone ring. I started down to answer it then realized that Daddy must have come to the house for something and was in the kitchen. I only heard his half of the conversation, so I didn't understand what was going on, but soon figured out who was on the other end of the line.

"Aw, come on, Josie," he said. He wasn't happy. Big surprise there. "What'd you do a thing like that for? I don't want—" She must have cut him off. Then he was silent, listening.

It became clear she wanted him to do something and he was trying to get out of it. Good luck with that. There probably wasn't a human being for four hundred miles in any direction who had ever told Josie Daniels no.

Daddy was quickly defeated. He finally gave up and said, "Uh-huh…" and then, "Uh-huh," again. "I've got three, maybe four. That should be plenty."

When he hung up the phone, I heard him rummaging around in the downstairs closets. Then he went out the kitchen door and into the garage that'd been attached to the old farm house when Daddy brought Mama home. There was no car in it. Daddy left his pickup sitting outside, and he'd told my grandparents to take Mama's car back to Tennessee after they'd brought me home in it.

I didn't hear the garage door open, so he didn't go anywhere, and he was soon back in the kitchen. I forgot all about it until the cars started arriving at our house. The plan had been that the men who'd done the tumbleweed chasing and painting would return tonight and assemble the tumbleweeds into "trees," tying them together with baling wire.

The first man who stepped out of his car was Samuel Pruitt, whose farm was on the other side of the county. He hadn't taken part in either the chasing or the painting. And he'd brought his wife and two kids.

While his wife was getting something out of the trunk of the car, another car arrived. Jose Vasquez had been at the chasing but not the painting. He got out with his family, too.

While the two women stood chatting, the kids, five or six of them, began chasing each other around the cars until Elena Vasquez told them to get up in the yard behind the yucca plant fence or they'd get run over. I looked up then and saw a line of cars coming down the road from the highway to the house.

Apparently, word about the Grand Tumbleweed Chase had spread. All the men who'd been there and a whole lot more, who hadn't been there but wished they had, were showing up to get in on the action in the final play of the game.

And their wives—led by Josie Daniels, I was sure—had turned the occasion into a potluck dinner. I wasn't certain how I felt about that, but it didn't matter one way or the other. She and the other women had taken over my house and hijacked my kitchen quicker than pirates boarding a merchant ship.

I stood at the front door like a cigar-store Indian, not knowing what to do or say as one woman after another bustled past me into the house with plates covered over with tinfoil and wrapped in towels. Men hauled long folding tables and metal folding chairs that must have come from the Fellowship Hall of the church out of the back of their pickups and carried them around the house to the garage. Everyone wanted to get a look at the tumbleweeds, of course. They were met at the door by a stern Jack Kavanagh, who informed them the men would have to wait until after supper when they went to work. And the women were banned from the barn altogether until everything was done and they were ready to select their "trees" to take home.

"How you doin, Bonnie?" said George Harper's wife, Melody. As she scurried past me, I caught the aroma of fried chicken seeping from under the covered dishes in her hands, and I suddenly realized I was not at all opposed to the goings-on in my house. No sir-eeee! A hot meal, a *home-cooked* meal—hey, for that I'd sign over the deed to the whole ranch.

After that, I stood at the front door, *smiling*, and greeted the women bearing foil- and towel-covered pans that smelled of baked ham and meatloaf, and bowls of pinto beans and potato salad, and acted as welcoming and friendly as if I'd been consulted about the whole thing all along. I could smell the jalapeños in whatever Juanita Ortega had prepared, and when the still-warm lemon meringue pie smell wafted from beneath Betty Prichard's wrappings, I almost drowned. I'd been looking forward to a frozen dinner—maybe the chicken one this time—for supper after the tumbleweeds had been cleared out of our barn.

Josie dispatched the deliveries here and there in the kitchen with the expertise of a five-star general organizing troop movements for an invasion. After a while, I abandoned my cigar-store Indian post and went to peek into the garage—which was not refrigerator cold, as it should have been, but toasty warm, courtesy of the space heaters Josie had directed Daddy to set up in there earlier in the day.

The food was placed on three long tables set end to end at the front of the garage, with tables lined up in diagonal rows in front of them all the way to the door. It was a good thing it was a two-car garage—another extravagance courtesy of my mother.

The thought stopped me. I'd never counted all the things Daddy had only done because Mama wanted them —the phone, the barn, the show ring, the horses, the garage, the—

Why had he bothered? I had to scramble then. Well… it had been done with his money, not his consent, and most of it he didn't like anyway. He'd get rid of it all eventually, just like he'd done with Mama's horses and paintings.

Josie caught sight of me and wiggled her finger in the universal come-here gesture. "I've got a package for you and your daddy out in the car," she said. "You need to go get it before I forget and take it back home with me."

Whenever we received a package in the mail, Spencer brought it to us as an excuse for a visit. Daddy subscribed to various catalogues—Sears and Wards, of course, but also places that sold saddles, bridles, stirrups and other tack for horses. Mama got catalogues, too, because the horses she trained used specialized equipment you couldn't find in regular stores. And she ordered most of her art supplies.

Spencer must have collected those packages at the post office and sent them back.

"It's a Christmas present from your grandparents."

I went out to their car and retrieved a package wrapped in brown shipping paper from the backseat. It was flat—only about two inches thick—but large—a rectangle that was about a foot and a half on one side and two feet on the other. I brought it into the house and stuck it behind the couch in the living room so it wouldn't get trampled by all the kids running around. And there were kids—in every shape and size. The little ones were underfoot no matter where you stepped. The older ones were herded into the parlor and warned on pain of death and dismemberment to "be good." Spencer stopped where he was hauling in tables long enough to catch his oldest grandson by the ear and pronounce, "You touch anything, I will snatch you bald-headed."

I wasn't relegated to the parlor like the other kids, but neither was I put to work in the kitchen with the women getting dinner ready. My place in the social order of things had changed since my mother died, and I had a foot in both worlds—adult and child. I didn't feel at all comfortable in either one.

It was hard to stay out of the way in the beehive of activity in the kitchen until I retreated into the alcove under the stairs to keep from bumping into trays of hot food. I didn't do it so I could eavesdrop on the women's conversations—and in the constant babble of talk, I couldn't have even if I'd wanted to. But since nobody noticed me there, I was a party to a candor they would never have expressed in my presence.

As the women bustled around to heat up the dishes that had gotten cold on the way out to my house, and to run an assembly line of yeast rolls through the oven, I caught snippets of hurried conversations. I quickly learned way more than I wanted to know about Mildred Fitzsimmons's hot flashes, Shirley Bracewell's hemorrhoids, and the perfume Mrs. Malone could swear she smelled on Mr. Malone's shirt.

Then I heard my mother's name and listened hard to what Charlene Noakes was saying to Wilma Kavanagh.

"…told him Rose was dead—how the North Koreans found out a thing like that, I don't know. Beau didn't believe them, of course, the way they lied about everything. But then he was released and found out it *was* true. Not surprising he…well…"

"Beau McGrath drove away from Muleshoe one man and came back three years later somebody else entirely," Josie Daniels said. Then she spoke so softly I had to strain to hear. "All those medals he came home with…he paid for every last one of them with a piece of his soul."

The medals I had put in a frame on top of the purple velvet from my Easter dress.

Chapter Sixteen

It was amazing how fast the dinner came together. In no time, Josie was calling out that supper was ready, and everyone dutifully filed into the garage to line up. Josie had pulled the food tables away from the wall to make room for lines on both sides. She thought of everything.

Pastor McGuiness said grace.

At the end of a list of thank-yous and we're-grateful-fors, he asked God to "Bless the hands that made this meal —" a one-beat pause "—and the ones that are about to make some Christmas trees."

Daddy didn't eat supper, or if he did, he ate it somewhere besides the garage. I caught part of a conversation between Josie and Spencer and heard Spencer say "...can't handle being crowded with a lot of people in a small space..." but I wasn't sure they were talking about Daddy.

As soon as supper was over, the women descended on the kitchen to clean up and to gossip, the kids were quarantined in the now empty space of the garage, and the men headed off to the barn to do the job they'd come to do. Many hands make light work—according to Pastor

McGuiness—and with so many people to help, assembling the trees wouldn't take long. I sneaked away as soon as I could to take my balcony seat above the show ring to watch.

Dozens of tumbleweeds dangled from their stems attached to the baling wire lines that ran the length of the ring. I knew a lot about paint—understood that the glaring green they'd dunked the weeds into would fade and mute as it dried. That was what happened to Mama's pictures. Shiny wet paint made colors pop out in a way dry paint never did.

But it didn't take but one look at the multihued green fuzzy balls in the glare of the overhead lights, hanging dry above small ponds of drizzled paint, to tell me this paint wasn't like Mama's. Wet or dry, the colors were jarring, bright and…harsh. I wasn't the only one who thought so.

"I thought they'd…you know…look better dry," George Harper said. "They're still so ugly they'd make a train take a dirt road."

Ed Baldwin had yelled at my daddy to "do something, *anything!*" at the board meeting and had stood in our front yard and listened to Daddy outline his plan. Then he'd gotten into his truck and driven away. He didn't show up for the painting, either, so this was his first look at the creations of Daddy's imagination.

He stood staring at them, then shook his head. "These things look like something my dog's been gnawing on under the porch. Do you actually expect us to take 'em home and put 'em in our living rooms?"

"You don't have to put anything in your living room, Ed," Daddy said. The vein in his temple had popped out and was throbbing. "You can take one and stick it up your—"

He caught himself in time, but it was a near thing.

"If you want a bare spot on your wall where a 'real' Christmas tree should be but isn't, that's fine by me. We don't need your help."

Mr. Baldwin turned and strode out of the show ring, his step so quick he kicked up little puffs of dust that hung in the air for a moment after he passed. He turned as he got to the door and you could tell he'd been thinking up a dramatic exit line.

"You know what you are, Beau? You're—"

"The man who's going to give you to the count of one to get out of my barn," Daddy said. The edge of menace in his voice was as sharp as a scythe. In that moment, he seemed like a very dangerous man.

As Mr. Baldwin stormed out, Daddy turned to the men standing in front of him.

"Nobody's holding a gun to your heads to get you to go along with this," he said. "You want to leave, there's the door. If you don't, we got a lot of work to do to put these things together so you can take your *trees* home with you tonight."

No one else left.

As before, Daddy had the whole thing organized. This time the men were in two-man teams. One man would hold the weeds in place while the other used baling wire to tie them together.

"We are *not* competing to see who can make the biggest Christmas tree," he said, and several of the men chuckled. "Most folks can't use a tree the size of a California redwood. We need little ones, too. All sizes and shapes. Fat ones. Skinny ones, short and tall."

Spencer unpinned a lime green weed from the line, then turned and took down a second weed that was the color of baby barf. He selected a small weed for the top of the tree that was as Army green as a Sherman tank.

"Might as well get creative," he said.

And they did—well, as creative as a bunch of cowboys could get.

George Harper and Frank Noakes made their first tree of eight small weeds. Four on the bottom, three above and then one on top. The whole thing was only about five feet tall. If it had been wrapped in silver foil, it could have passed for a giant candy kiss.

Pete Prichard made half a dozen trees with the same color combination. He and Rufus Fitzsimmons used John Deere green for the big weed at the bottom, baby puke in the middle and stomped bug on top.

Harry Malone and Damien Duncan made several tall, thin trees that wouldn't stand up on their own—but Daddy said that might be just the shape somebody wanted, and if they did, they'd have to figure out some kind of "tree stand" to keep them from falling over.

Charlie Bracewell and Jack Kavanagh enlisted Billy Hennessy's help to construct the big tree for in front of the courthouse. It had five weeds on the bottom, four above that, then three, two and one on top. It stood fifteen feet tall and twenty wide, and when they were finished, the other men burst into spontaneous applause.

Somebody'd have to haul it into town in a cotton trailer.

When I saw that most of the weeds had been assembled into trees, I sneaked back out of the show ring and was in the kitchen helping to dry the last of the supper dishes when Spencer stepped inside and announced that the job was done and we could all have a look.

The trees took up two-thirds of the space in the show ring. The other end of the ring slowly filled up with people. They were bunched together, none of them venturing too near the green weeds. Many in the crowd were as anxious to get a look at Daddy's mythical heated show ring as they were the Christmas trees. The crowd fell into what felt like an awed silence as soon as the people stepped into the ring with the creations, whether shocked into silence by the trees or the ring, I didn't know.

Some of the trees were as tall as a man; others were short and squatty. Not a single one of the stickery green weeds bore even the vaguest resemblance to a real Christmas tree. It looked like that whole end of the show ring was occupied by an invading army of green snowmen.

Nobody spoke. The silence drew out and felt awkward.

"What do you think?" Spencer tossed the words out into the middle of the crowd like a hand grenade.

I looked over at Daddy, expecting to see a stony un-expression, or perhaps the vein in his temple throbbing. That wasn't what I saw. Maybe it was a trick of the shadowy overhead lighting, but if I'd seen that look on the face of any other human being, I'd have called the look fear. It was gone in a flash and the mask was pulled down over his features again. I'd just imagined it. I had to have imagined it.

"They're...uh...they're sure green alright," Melody Harper said.

The words hung with the dust in the air that'd been stirred up when the people came into the ring. No one else spoke. The wind whistled outside in the darkness. The building groaned and creaked around us. Feet shifted on the bare ground.

"Why, Spencer Daniels! Use your eyes, man." Josie pushed her way through the crowd, chattering as she came.

"Over there," she said, pointing to a little tree that was a bright John Deere green. It stood near the door into the horse stalls and tack room where I'd sneaked in and out.

"That one. Just look at it. Why, it's just the right size to fit between the window and the china cabinet. You better set it aside right now."

She paused then and turned to look pointedly into the faces of the women in the crowd.

"We're not likely to find another Christmas tree anywhere else that'll fit half as nice."

After that, it was downhill all the way.

The wives set to sizing up the trees, mentally placing them against imaginary walls and next to imaginary pianos.

Daddy had done it. He'd won.

But I wasn't disappointed. And I didn't know why.

I looked for him, but couldn't locate him anywhere. Then I spotted him. He had taken Rufus Fitzsimmons by the arm, pulled him aside, and was engaged in earnest conversation with him. Then the two of them left through the breezeway toward the barn.

Chapter Seventeen

I SUPPOSED Daddy would be right back so we could select our tree. I waited. And waited. But he didn't return.

As the trees were carried one by one out of our show barn and hauled away in pickup trucks, tied on top of cars or poking out of trunks held closed over them with baling wire, nobody noticed his absence but me. The later it got, the more anxious I got—not because I wanted to see him or anything like that. But as the Christmas trees were selected, the pickings began to get a bit slim. Oh, there'd still be plenty to hand out on the lot next to the church, but all the really good ones were soon long gone. What was left behind in the show barn when everybody but Spencer and Josie had left looked like the half-price table at an Army surplus store.

"Where's your daddy?" Spencer asked as he pulled his knit cap down to his eyebrows so he wouldn't freeze his bald head in the wind.

"He left," I said. "We never got to pick our tree."

"Oh, you got a tree alright. He picked it out soon's we

got it assembled. He set it aside, took it and put it in one of the horse stalls in the barn." He walked with me out of the show ring into the barn. "It's a big one, way taller than your daddy, made out of three perfectly round trees. Don't know how in the world he intends to get that thing in the house."

He pointed to a horse stall, and I raced to it and flung open the door.

The horse stall was empty.

Spencer came up behind me and looked into the stall, confused. "I thought it was this stall, but maybe…"

I ran to the next stall as Spencer kept babbling.

"The tumbleweeds he picked were all painted right at the end, when they had to pour all the leftover paint together—all the different colors—to have enough to get the last ones."

I flung open the door of that stall. No tree.

"And they figured out then they should have mixed all the paint together right at the beginning because the mixture was the best color green of them all. Kind of a spruce green. Real pretty."

I pulled open the door of the next stall. No tree.

"It looked very natural…"

Spencer went on about how natural it looked as I went from one stall to the next all the way down the side of the barn. Looked in every one. There wasn't a tree in any of them.

Spencer had stopped talking, confused.

"I don't know what to tell you, sweetheart," he said. "I could have sworn he picked out something special."

"Oh, any one of those leftover trees will do," I said. "What difference does it make? A tree's a tree, right?"

"I'm sure he'll get…the best tree he can find."

I wasn't sure of that at all. He'd let everybody else have the good trees and didn't even think about a tree for us. For *me*. I turned and ran out of the barn into the house, up to my bedroom and threw myself on my bed in tears.

Chapter Eighteen

WHEN DADDY GOT HOME a few hours later, I pretended I was asleep. I heard the truck drive up in front and had plenty of time to clean everything up and put it away, hop into bed and act like I'd been asleep for hours. I hadn't been, though. I'd been sitting up in bed, going through the contents of my Close Your Eyes box.

Inside it were things that'd belonged to Mama.

It had all happened so fast. As soon as they learned Daddy was "going to war *again*," Grampa and Grandma Cresswell launched a campaign to get Mama to come home to Black Saddle Farm in Tennessee to live with them while he was gone. Mama said no, absolutely not. She might have been tempted, though. I don't know. It'd sure have been easier than staying in Texas. Mama's parents weren't "rich," but they were "wealthy." There was a subtle difference between the two that was totally lost on me. Mama tried to explain it to me once, how in the society of Tompkinsburg, Tennessee, being "rich" was…unseemly, but all the old families were wealthy, living in their stately houses with big yards and towering shade trees while the "help" cooked the meals and cleaned up the messes.

Grandma spent months doing her dead-level best to change Mama's mind. For a tiny woman—Dorothy Cresswell wouldn't have weighed a hundred pounds with three running jumps at the scales—there was steel sheathed in her soft voice. The original velvet hammer, she was relentlessly persistent.

Mama told Grandma she had to stay in Texas to take care of her horses. Of course, any of the ranch hands could have cared for the animals—in Texas, a horse is a horse—but they were Mama's babies, and she wasn't about to turn their care over to somebody else.

And there was the ranch to run—*thousands* of acres. Mama had crops to raise, fences to mend, cattle to see to. She didn't perform any of those tasks, of course. The ranch foreman and other ranch hands did. But to hear her tell Grandma, she was in the saddle all day, sunup to sundown, a branding iron in one hand and a cotton plant in the other. The truth was, Mama flat out didn't want to live anywhere but west Texas. She loved the High Plains with a passion totally lost on those who'd lived all their lives there. And besides, she'd promised Daddy she'd "take care of things" while he was gone, and she intended to honor that promise.

So we stayed in Texas. But we visited my grandparents a couple of times a year, and it was on the trip the summer before last, in July 1952, that Mama got sick.

"It's just a cold," Mama tells Grandma, who's fluttering around her like a little bird. Mama's voice sounds funny because her nose is clogged up. "Quit fussing over me."

Grandma ignores her, pours Kentucky bourbon into a shot glass, adds a spoonful of honey and makes Mama drink it.

"This'll open up your sinuses," she says.

Mama turns the glass up and swallows the contents. "Whew!" she gasps, sputtering and coughing. "You could drive a bus through my sinuses now. Another couple of those and I'll be too drunk to care."

The next day, Mama's cold is worse. Grandma smears Mentholatum on her chest, something else to open up her sinuses, and forces her to drink, like, half a gallon of orange juice. Mama won't eat anything, though. She's not hungry.

As I come down the stairs to breakfast the next morning, I hear Mama in her first-floor bedroom coughing. It's an awful, barking sound. I rush to her room, but Grandma catches me at the door and shoos me out, saying I need to let Mama rest.

Dr. Abercrombie comes to the house after lunch and stays in Mama's bedroom a long time. When he comes out, he stands by the bedroom door, talking to Grandma. I hear the word bronchitis, *and he tells her he'll write some prescriptions for Mama.*

"She'll be fine in a couple of days," he says.

But she isn't fine in a couple of days. I wake up every morning now with a knot in my belly so big I don't want breakfast. I'm scared to death all the time, but I don't know what I'm afraid of.

The doctor comes back every day to give Mama shots, and Grandma hires a nurse named Belle to stay with Mama around the clock. Now the coughing I hear coming from her room isn't a barking sound. It's a clogged, gurgling sound and it goes on and on and on.

Grandma allows me in Mama's room once a day and only lets me stay long enough to give Mama a peck on the cheek and tell her I love her. Mama looks shrunken in the bed, her hair a tangle around her head. Her skin is so pale her eyes look like bruises on her face.

After breakfast one morning, Grandpa tells me to "go outside and play," like there's something to do all by myself in a huge empty yard. Then I spot a tree with a limb on the bottom low enough for me to grab.

I've never climbed a tree in my life. I've read about it, though, how other kids make tree-house forts where they keep a supply of dirt clods to beat back attacks by earthbound kids like me. I take hold of the low-hanging limb and begin to clamber up into the branches, going higher and higher into the leaves. It's glorious up here! I feel like I do when I stand at my window and pretend to be a ship captain. I'm on top of the world and I—

"Bonnie!" It's Belle, Mama's nurse. "Bonnie, where are you?"

"Here, in the tree," I call down. She looks up, but I don't think she sees me.

"Get down out of there," she says. "Your mother's calling for you."

That's when I discover it's a whole lot harder to climb down a tree than up one. I finally make it to the low limb, jump off onto the ground and race into the house.

Into chaos.

Mama can't breathe!

Belle has called an ambulance that has just pulled up out front. Grandma is rushing around, giving orders, doing I don't know what. I catch one word of her frantic babble. I don't know what the word means, but the very sound of it is chilling. Pneumonia.

As the ambulance attendants open the back bay doors of the big white truck and begin pulling out a stretcher, Mama spots me in the doorway and motions me to her.

"You be a good girl," she gasps.

She doesn't say "while I'm gone" or "until I get back." Just be a good girl.

I'm suddenly so frightened I'm the one who can't breathe, and I grab her hand, determined not to let go no matter what.

"I want to go with you," I plead. "Please."

She pats my hand weakly. "I'll never leave you," she says. Who said anything about leaving *me? Sudden terror pounds through my chest like a freight train. "Just close your eyes," she says. Gasp. "I'll always be there."*

I want to say something, anything, but I burst into tears instead and sit there holding her hand, sobbing. The ambulance attendants come into the room to load her on the stretcher, but I won't let go of her hand. I'm afraid if I do—

They have to pry my fingers off Mama's, and by then I'm hysterical, crying and wailing. Belle has to drag me out of the room and then sits in the chair in the hallway with her arms wrapped tight around me as they wheel Mama out past me.

"Mama! Mama!" I cry. "Mommeee!"

She looks my way and smiles. But the smile looks sad, somehow. Then she is gone.

Grandma comes home briefly the next morning to gather up some of Mama's things to take back to the hospital.

"I'll get the blue nightgown with the white flowers—that's Mama's favorite," I say. I rush to the dresser to find it. I'm stuffing it into the top of the bag when the phone rings. Grandma goes out into the hall to answer it. Then she screams, a wail as thin as a paper cut.

Chapter Nineteen

I LIVED with my grandparents for nine months after Mama died until Daddy got home. I longed for that day, ached for it. My daddy would make everything right! He would lift me up into his arms and hold me so tight that the awful empty place inside me would be filled up again.

He returned from Korea in October, but was in a veterans hospital in Virginia for three months after that, and I pleaded with my grandparents to take me there to visit him. Every time I asked, they looked uncomfortable and said it wasn't the kind of hospital where you could have visitors.

We spent Christmas together, just the three of us. I don't have a single memory of it.

My grandparents drove us to Muleshoe in early February. When we got to the ranch, Daddy was standing on the front porch, waiting for us. I leapt out of the car, ran up the sidewalk and launched myself at him—grabbing him around the waist and squeezing with the strength of the pent-up desperation that'd been building in me for months.

It was like hugging a flagpole.

The next day, I heard my grandparents pleading with Daddy to let them take me back home with them "just for a little while, Beau…until you get back on your feet."

Daddy didn't argue. He didn't say anything except, "She's all I've got."

They left two days later, after we scattered Mama's ashes.

*The wind is blowing. Mama loves the wind. Lov*ed *the wind. As the four of us walk together out into the prairie behind our house, I see her long hair floating in the wind behind her like a gossamer shawl.* You always have to face the wind. *That's what she told me.* If you don't, it'll blow your hair into your eyes and you can't see. Look into the wind, sweetheart, and it's like you're flying!

There are tears on my cheeks. I must be crying, but I don't feel it. I don't feel anything except hollow and empty. Grandpa has tears on his cheeks, too, and Grandma is leaning against him as they walk— like he's almost holding her up—and she's crying softly.

Daddy's face is as blank as a mannequin.

Then he stops and takes the jar—Grandma calls it an urn—in both hands in front of him. He holds it out to me, but I don't know why.

"Take the lid off, honey," Grandma says, her voice tear clotted.

I take the lid off and Daddy holds the jar out again, as if he's about to tip it over.

"Wait!" Grandpa says. "You can't just dump…shouldn't we say something?"

Daddy stands there holding the urn as Grandma speaks, crying as she talks, saying how much she'll miss her precious "baby girl." She's standing right beside me, but I'm having trouble hearing what she's saying. It's not that the wind is blowing her words away. A great roaring sound has started inside my head, and I can't hear much of anything through it.

Grandpa speaks. Then everyone is quiet, and I realize it must be my turn. I say, "I love you, Mama," but I can't hear the words.

Then Daddy turns the urn upside down and a gray cloud flows out of it—Mama!—and instantly vanishes in the wind. We walk slowly back to the house. Daddy hasn't spoken a single word.

The night after my grandparents left was when I made the Close Your Eyes box. While Daddy sat in the parlor, just sat, staring at something on the wall across from him that I couldn't see, I went around the too-quiet house gathering up items to put in an orange crate I'd found in the garage.

Hair combs from Mama's bathroom.

The necklace Daddy gave her for her birthday out of her jewelry box.

A scarf from her closet that still had a whiff of her perfume on it if you held it tight up against your nose and inhaled deeply.

I picked up things I could picture her wearing or using or just holding. My little white clutch purse that matched the dress with blue flowers—we'd driven to Lubbock to get it the Easter before Daddy left. The big spoon out of the kitchen drawer she used to stir chili with, and her apron that had a stain on the front—chocolate from the last batch of fudge. The curry comb from the barn she used to groom the horses and a piece of leather from Twosy's bridle. When I had the box full, I went into my room and closed the door, climbed up into the middle of my bed, and set the box in front of me. Then I reached into the box, took out the pallet with a multicolored smear of dried paint, closed my eyes, and remembered Mama at her easel, capturing the silver glow of the harvest moon.

I didn't often open the Close Your Eyes box—it was a double-edged sword that cut into my heart with longing as it warmed me inside with a sense of her presence. But that wasn't why I only brought the box out of the back of my closet once in a while. In my mind, every one of the items in that box glowed with my mother's essence, and touching them imparted some essential part of her to me. It was precious beyond measure, that glow, and I feared to use it up, like watching a candle burn down until it finally gutters out and is gone. I hoarded my candle and only lit it when I really needed the warmth and light.

And I had needed that warmth tonight.

When I heard the door to my room open, I saw the hallway light through a forest of eyelashes and Daddy's silhouette framed in the doorway. He stood there for a while, like he always did. Not saying anything, just standing there. Then he closed the door and went away. I thought about the scraggly green weeds in the barn that would be our Christmas tree because Daddy hadn't bothered to save a good one for us, and I cried myself to sleep.

Chapter Twenty

DADDY WOKE me up the next morning right after sunrise by knocking on my door. He didn't come into the room, though, just called through the door that he had to go into town on business and he'd be back in the middle of the morning. I'd gotten so little sleep the night before that I rolled over and dozed off and didn't wake up until I heard the pickup pull up—not out front but on the far side of the house. That was odd.

Maybe it was because of the snow. It had picked up overnight. Spencer would say, "B'lieve it's gettin' serious now." The flakes were no longer big and fluffy, floating down out of the sky. They were smaller, falling fast, almost like rain. The yard was already buried in three, maybe four inches of it, and it didn't show any signs of letting up. I heard the kitchen door open a few minutes later, and Daddy called out to me from the foot of the stairs.

"Bonnie, where are you?"

Where did he think I was? Cleveland?

"I'm in my room, Daddy. I still have my pajamas on, but I'll get dressed and come down and make breakfast," meaning I'd set out bowls and the milk, sugar and cereal boxes.

"No," he said. "Don't come down. Stay in your room."

"Why?" I called out, but the kitchen door opened and closed, and I wasn't sure he heard me.

As I put on my jeans and pulled up my boots, I heard him come into the house again through the front door. I heard a clunk, like something had fallen over—maybe a lamp. What could Daddy possibly be doing that involved breaking things in the living room?

There was silence after that. I stood at my door, my ear to the crack, wanting to sneak down the hall and stairs and see what was going on. But I didn't.

"You can come down now," he finally called up. "I'll have Frosted Flakes this morning instead of Cheerios."

Something about his voice was odd, too. Off somehow.

I went down into the kitchen to find him standing by the table with the all-too-familiar blank expressionless face. But it was different somehow. Like there was movement underneath. Almost like he was *trying* not to have any kind of look on his face. He was covered with snowflakes. Hunks of white clung to his clothing from head to foot, and pieces of it had fallen off onto the kitchen floor. Big pieces of snow, in fact, were lying all over the floor between him and the closed door of the living room.

There was something not right about that, too, but I couldn't put my finger on what it was.

"I brought in our Christmas tree and set it up in the living room," he said.

"Goody," I said and turned to the cabinet where the cereal was kept.

"Aren't you excited to see it?" He seemed genuinely confused.

"Excited? What for? I saw the leftovers in the barn last

night after you gave trees to everybody else. There was nothing there to get excited about."

"You think I gave all the good trees to everybody else?"

"You *did* give all the good trees to everybody else." I hadn't meant to allow the hurt in my voice.

He took a step toward me then stopped when I cringed away.

"Just…go take a look."

Fine. Get it over with.

I pushed open the swinging door into the living room, where our Christmas trees always stood in front of the window that looked out on the prairie. What I saw didn't make any sense. It was a tumbleweed Christmas tree, alright, made of three perfectly round tumbleweeds—the one on the bottom was surely the big kahuna we'd snagged during the chase. The top of the "tree" almost brushed the twelve-foot ceiling.

It wasn't John Deere green, though, baby puke green or smashed-bug green. It wasn't green at all.

It was white.

The whole tree was covered in snow.

I looked back at Daddy.

"But…it'll melt!"

Daddy laughed, a full, hearty bellowing laugh like I hadn't heard in a long time. "No, it won't. Touch it."

I crossed the room in a daze and put out my hand, one finger extended to a snow-covered limb. What I touched wasn't cold. It was puffy, as soft as…

"It's cotton," Daddy said. "Cotton lint. I cornered Rufus last night and did some arm-twisting, got him to agree to let me take this tree over to the gin and set it in the processing room. It was there all night…just gathering lint."

I pulled off a small piece of pure, white snow. Cotton

lint. I turned back to Daddy and blurted out the first thing that came into my head. "But…why?"

"You love snow."

I just looked at him and couldn't quite seem to get words out. "For *me*?"

"Snow makes ugly things beautiful. That's what you said."

I didn't even know he'd heard me.

He chuckled then. "And if ever there was anything on God's earth that's butt ugly, it's a tumbleweed painted green."

I still couldn't get my mind around it. "You did this *for me*, because I like snow?"

He nodded; then he got that look in his eyes I had come to hate, the faraway look that meant he'd crawled into a hole and pulled the dirt in after him. And left me behind. But this time he came back.

"And because…"

It was clear he absolutely, one hundred percent did NOT want to say what he was about to say. But he kept talking.

"Your mother…always liked snow, too."

Chapter Twenty-One

WE SPENT the rest of the day decorating the tree.

The Christmas lights looked like a clot of dead spiders in the box. Daddy took them out and untangled them, placing them in three lines on the floor, and plugged them into the wall socket. None of the strings lit up. He tinkered around with bulbs, replacing them, swapping them from string to string until he finally got one string of red bulbs to light up. It would have to do. We weren't likely to be going into town for new lights, not in the blizzard that was raging outside.

Then we got out the boxes of decorations and began hanging them on the tree. Okay, *placing* them on the tree. There was no space between a tumbleweed's limbs like on a spruce or pine tree, where decorations could dangle. Attaching a Christmas decoration to a cotton-covered tumbleweed was akin to pinning a merit badge on a Boy Scout's chest.

Inside the big box of glass balls and plastic snowflakes was a smaller box. Daddy picked it up, opened it and stood for a moment, not moving. He stared at the contents like it was a box full of rattlesnakes. It was obvious he didn't want to touch it. When he turned and wordlessly handed it to me, I understood. The decorations in the box were so delicate he didn't want to touch them because he didn't want to be responsible for breaking one! The decorations were made of eggshells. And they'd been fragile even before they'd sat in a box for years.

I picked up the first one out of the box by the loop of sewing thread on top. It was supposed to be one of the three wise men, but the crown made out of aluminum foil was smashed, and the cotton that formed his beard had come loose so it dangled off the right side of his face beneath his Magic Marker-drawn mouth.

"We need some Elmer's," I said and hopped up and went into the kitchen to find some.

As soon as I had the beard securely affixed to the shell again, I held it up in the air and closed my eyes.

Mama.

I don't remember the first ones she made. I was too young. By the time I was old enough to help with the process, we already had a box full of them. There were Santa Claus eggs and Mrs. Santa Claus eggs. Four or five sets of three kings. Most of the eggs were just decorated like ornaments, with sequins and pieces of red and green ribbon glued all over them.

But Mama had removed one side of some eggs so they formed shadowboxes. She covered the jagged edges where she'd pecked away the eggshells with colored rickrack, then squirted glue into the opening, swished it all around the inside of the shell and poured glitter in after it. Later, when she dumped out the glitter that didn't stick, the inside of the egg sparkled, and she'd set something tiny inside—a silver ball of crushed foil or kernels of dried corn painted bright colors.

The first time she allowed me to participate, I had to stand on a chair to be the right height in front of the kitchen counter.

"You have to make a hole in both ends of the egg," she said and began to peck a toothpick gently against one end of the egg in her hand. "It's hard not to crack the shell—"

And that was exactly what she did. So she took another egg out of the carton and went to work on it, and this time she was able to peck a hole in the shell. Then she turned the egg over and began pecking on the other end.

Tap, tap, tap.

Mama bent over her work with a look of concentration that pleated between her eyebrows. Her long hair flowed over her shoulders and fell all the way to the counter. I thought then, as I had thought so many times before, that she looked like a princess. My mother was the most beautiful woman in the world.

Once she had holes poked in both ends of the shell, she stuck the toothpick through a hole and wiggled it around inside the shell "to break the yoke and mix it all up with the egg white."

She held the egg over a bowl, put her lips to the hole on one end and began to blow. Nothing happened for a few seconds, so she blew harder. A bit of egg began to drip out of the hole on the bottom. Then a little more. Suddenly, the rest of the egg came out in a whoosh and plopped into the bowl.

The empty eggshell was placed in a box, and we went to work on another egg.

It was years before I was allowed to try my hand at emptying the eggshells. In the beginning, I broke every egg I tried. But I gradually got the hang of it.

I opened my eyes and stared at the wise-man eggshell in my hand. I was acutely aware as I placed it oh so carefully on the tree that if I broke it, there'd be no replacement. These eggshell decorations were all there'd ever be.

I stopped and held my breath. Not necessarily.

Daddy and I didn't talk much as we decorated the tree. I didn't want to say anything for fear of snapping the fragile bond between us that felt as tenuous as a single strand of spiderweb. I thought Daddy was being careful, too.

When we were done, we stepped back to inspect our work. The tree needed popcorn and cranberry strings. Our trees always had those, and linked chains of colored construction paper, and candy canes. We didn't have any candy canes or cranberries—maybe a few sheets of construction paper stuffed in a folder somewhere in the attic boxes that contained what had been in Mama's studio. It would take all day to find it. We had a jar of popping corn in the cabinet, but I wasn't sure I could make it without burning the house down.

One good thing about a tumbleweed Christmas tree. There was no problem getting the star to stay put on top. Ours was a gold ceramic one that Mama had made, and all Daddy had to do was set it on top of the tree.

"I bet our tree is the prettiest tree in the county," Daddy said.

"Of course it is," I said. "All the others are some shade of puke green."

He smiled at me for that. Then he went out to do chores.

As soon as he was gone, I went into the kitchen and took out a box of eggs and a jar of toothpicks. There were only seven eggs, and I broke the first three I worked on. I managed to get the egg blown out of the fourth shell, but it cracked when I tried to peck out the side of it. The fifth egg was the charm. It held together when I pecked a hole in the side to reveal the interior.

I dug around in Mama's art supplies in the attic for some paint, searched until I found the exact color I wanted —John Deere green. I got a small jar of silver glitter, then went downstairs and broke off a limb of the tumbleweed and pulled off the cotton to reveal the green stick beneath. As soon as the empty eggshell's glittering silver interior was dry, I used little pieces of broken stick to construct a mini tumbleweed inside the eggshell. It didn't look much like a tumbleweed, but I had done the best I could do.

That was when I felt it. No, *didn't* feel it. It had been there for so long it felt normal—but now the open airy feeling in my belly was gone.

Chapter Twenty-Two

I MADE myself a peanut butter and jelly sandwich for supper. Daddy had a meatloaf frozen dinner and a bowl of Campbell's Chicken Noodle Soup, then took his coffee into the living room. I followed and sat down in front of the tree, which looked better in the lamplit room than it had this afternoon. In the dim light, you could almost believe we had a snow-covered Christmas tree in our living room.

I noticed that Daddy must have sneaked up to his bedroom while I was eating my sandwich because the present for me he'd been hiding in his closet was now under the tree. I knew what it was. Daddy wasn't very good at hiding things, and I'd seen the Betsy Wetsy doll box before he wrapped it.

I'd gotten Daddy three pairs of socks almost a month ago when I'd gone shopping with Josie. Actually, she had gotten them for me to "give your daddy." As I'd wrapped the cereal box with the socks inside in brown paper from grocery sacks, I had considered cutting the threads in the toe of every sock so it'd fray and make a hole. Thinking about that made me feel uncomfortable now…sitting in front of the snow-covered tree Daddy'd gotten just for me. Well, I'd made a Christmas surprise for him, too.

I opened the drawer where I'd put the decoration I'd made that afternoon. "Close your eyes. It's a surprise."

Daddy dutifully closed his eyes. I went to stand in front of him and dangled the egg from the sewing thread on top.

"Okay. Open your eyes. Merry Christmas."

Daddy opened his eyes and stared at the ornament. Instead of smiling, though, his face froze in place, and I felt the familiar cold chill down my spine. When he reached out and took the eggshell, his face was an expressionless mask.

"Your mother made these every Christmas," he said, in a toneless voice, like he was telling me my shoe was untied.

Then I got it! Daddy hadn't liked the eggshell decorations when Mama made them! Any more than he'd liked the yucca plants she'd set out around the yard! Or her horses. Or…I'd seen it on his face when he opened the box. He wouldn't even touch them and made me hang them because he really didn't want them on the tree at all. And he'd get rid of them, too, just like he'd gotten rid of Toastie and Tater and Mama's paintings. When he did, he'd throw mine out with the rest of them.

He made an effort to rearrange his features, but it was a lost cause.

"It's real pretty," he lied. Then he stood and hung it on the tree—up high near the star so you didn't have to look at it if you didn't want to.

The wind whistled outside in the silence that followed, and blew through the big hole that had reopened in my belly. The familiar emptiness had returned, and I knew then that it would always be there, that I'd been a fool to believe it would ever go away.

Daddy draped a phony smile on his face like hanging a

sheet on a clothesline. He must have felt the gap reopen, too, though, and maybe he was finally figuring out what I already knew. There wasn't any way to close the hole, so give it up. Stop struggling. Life was easier when you didn't care.

Then I remembered the box Josie had given me the night before.

"I forgot to tell you—we got something from Grandma and Grampa. I stuck it behind the couch."

I hauled it out and handed it to him. He took it to put under the tree with the other gifts. Then stopped, staring at it. I came closer to see what he was looking at. There was something written on the brown wrapping paper in my grandmother's beautiful cursive script. I hadn't noticed it last night.

When I got close enough to read it, I froze, too.

"Bonnie Leigh," it said, "this is a Christmas present from your mother."

Without a word, I grabbed the box out of Daddy's hands and began to tear into it. The outside was wrapped in brown shipping paper, but under that was a real Christmas present done up in silver wrapping paper, red ribbon and a bow. A smashed bow. Taped next to the bow was a Christmas card.

I pulled the envelop free and opened the card.

"Read it out loud," Daddy said.

"This gift isn't from Harold and me," I read in a trembling voice. "It's from my precious Rose."

The words knocked the wind out of me, like I'd been thrown from a horse. I gripped the card tight in my hands, but I had suddenly forgotten how to read.

Daddy pulled the card gently away and continued. His voice sounded raw. Hoarse, full of pebbles. Like he'd clamped down on his vocal cords and they could barely move.

"She worked on it every afternoon the whole time the two of you were here, while Harold and I tried to keep you occupied so you wouldn't see."

That was why Grampa had developed the sudden obsession with Monopoly, and why Grandma had always seemed to need my help in the kitchen when she was baking.

"I remember!" I blurted out. "Grandpa had to stop playing one afternoon because he got a phone call—and I already had Boardwalk, Park Place and the railroads anyway—so I went to see Mama while he was talking. When she spotted me, she jumped up and spun me around and marched me back out of the room. She said I couldn't see what she was working on, that it was a surprise." I had forgotten all about that. Mama had gotten sick a couple of days later, and like rot spreading through an apple from one black spot, the memories of that had turned all the time near them dark.

"I watched over her shoulder while she worked," Daddy read, and I could picture my little grandmother fluttering around my mother like a hummingbird. "I always loved to watch her paint. And she'd look up at me and smile and say she couldn't wait to see your face and your daddy's when you saw this painting."

"It isn't finished," Grandma wrote. "She never had a chance to complete it. I've held onto it all these months, saving it to send when the two of you were together. Merry Christmas, Beau and Bonnie…from Rose."

Daddy looked up from the card in his hands and his eyes locked on mine. Then Daddy knelt down on the floor beside me and the two of us pulled away the wrapping paper together—slowly, reverently.

The painting was one of Mama's whimseys, like the one where she and I and Daddy are eating Thanksgiving dinner inside a turkey, or where she and Daddy are trying to pull me out of a gob of chewing gum the size of a car.

We aren't inside a turkey in this one, though. Daddy and I are *here,* in this room—with the big leather couch draped in a turquoise Indian blanket we got the time we went to Ruidoso. The recliner and end table are beside it. The pole lamp is turned on. So is the lamp on the table between the two flowered wingback chairs in the back of the room across from the big window that looks out on the prairie. Daddy and I have our backs turned, facing that window. We're holding hands. He is in his Marine Corps dress uniform—blue jacket, red trim and gold buttons on the shoulders, white hat and belt, and the crease in his pants is sharp enough to slice bread. I am wearing the Easter dress with tiny blue flowers and holding the little white clutch purse we got in Lubbock. My hair is pulled back by the blue headband Mama decorated with the black rose off her hat.

The bottom left of the picture is the part that isn't complete. It's Mama, sitting on the arm of one of the wingback chairs. All the details are missing. There's only the base color and a roughed-in drawing on top. Little more than a sketch. You can see through it to the flowered upholstery of the chair. But faint as the image is, you can still tell Mama is looking at us. And that we are looking at what stands between us and that big window.

It's a giant white snowman decorated like a Christmas tree—*right here in our living room*. It has lights strung around it, bright red ones. There's a ceramic star sitting on the top that brushes the ceiling, and little blue, yellow, green and purple decorations scattered all across its surface.

I heard Daddy gasp. Or maybe it was me. I couldn't

tell which. Daddy stood up slowly and held the painting out in trembling hands, looking from the painting to the tree and back to the painting.

The decorations on the snowman are just suggested, not detailed, little blobs of color like fall leaves on a tree. All but one of them, that is. Up near the top beneath the star is an oval decoration—small, the size of an egg— painted bright John Deere green. There's a cotton-edged opening in the side of the decoration that reveals a sparkling interior, glittering silver like snow in the moonlight. In the center of it is what looks like a miniature tumbleweed.

"Daddy…?"

I was about to cry. And to laugh. About to be sick. About to leap up and run out of the room. I didn't do any of those things. I just looked with Daddy at the painting. At the tree. At the painting again.

I sensed movement next to me and saw Daddy out of the corner of my eye, turning as I was turning, to the back corner of the room where in the painting a transparent figure is perched on the arm of the wingback chair. I wanted her to be there so bad my heart ripped out of my chest with longing. But she wasn't, of course. I felt Daddy tense next to me and stop breathing. When he slowly let out the breath, it carried with it a sound. A soft sound, a strangled sob.

Daddy'd wanted her to be there, too. Just as bad as I did.

"How could she…?" I didn't finish. I didn't have any air in my lungs to speak, and there was no answer to how could she, anyway. She couldn't. Except she did.

I looked again at the picture and turned back to face the tree. Daddy did, too.

We stood there together.

Then Daddy reached out and took my hand. Just like

Mama had painted it. My small hand fit snug into his big one. His fingers felt warm and strong curled around mine. I'd have smiled, but I couldn't. My lip was trembling, and tears were running down my cheeks. When I looked up at Daddy, there were tears streaming down his cheeks, too.

Then he squeezed my hand.

I squeezed back as hard as I could.

THE END

A Note from the Author

Thank you for reading *Tumbleweed Christmas.*

If you enjoyed this book. would you please consider writing a review of it on Amazon so other readers might enjoy it too. Just a couple of sentences. That would mean a lot to me.

Thank you!

Ninie Hammon

Want More?

Get a FREE copy of my best selling novel *Five Days in May* when you sign up to my VIP mailing list.

Go to: http://sterlingandstone.net/9e-free-book

Also by Ninie Hammon

The Unexplainable Collection

Five Days in May

Black Sunshine

The Based on True Stories Collection

Home Grown

Sudan

When Butterflies Cry

The Knowing Series

The Knowing

The Deceiving

The Reckoning

Stand-alone Psychological Thrillers

The Memory Closet

The Last Safe Place

Nonfiction/Memoir

Typin' 'Bout My Generation

Made in the USA
Coppell, TX
02 December 2019

12276369R00074